IDLE HANDS

CASSONDRA WINDWALKER

AGORA BOOKS

ABOUT THE AUTHOR

Cassondra Windwalker grew up on plains and longed for mountains. Today she lives by the frozen sea. She earned a BA of Letters at the University of Oklahoma and pursued careers in bookselling and law enforcement before resigning her post to write full time.

A poet, essayist, and novelist, her short-form work has appeared in numerous literary journals and art books. Her full-length books of poetry and prose are available in bookstores and online. She welcomes conversations with readers through her social media platforms and in the occasional coffee shop.

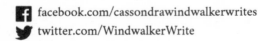

facebook.com/cassondrawindwalkerwrites
twitter.com/WindwalkerWrite

ALSO BY CASSONDRA WINDWALKER

IDLE HANDS

CASSONDRA WINDWALKER

First published in Great Britain in 2020 by Agora Books

Agora Books is a division of Peters Fraser + Dunlop Ltd

55 New Oxford Street, London WC1A 1BS

Printed and bound in Great Britain by Clays Ltd, Elcograf S.p.A.

To my father, who taught me to play tennis, save the brakes, and play a mean devil's advocate

PROLOGUE

PROLOGUE

Of all of them, Tad was the hardest for me to hold on to. Perhaps that was why I let him go so soon.

You probably know a little about light theory. Or rather, the absence of a satisfactory theory to explain one of the most fundamental necessities of your paltry existence. According to your scientists, it's either a wave that thinks it's a particle, or a particle that thinks it's a wave. I never tire of listening to you fight to tie up ideas in words. To be fair, I suppose that's not your fault. You're limited that way. You can't comprehend a thought you can't assign a name to.

Of course, light is especially difficult for you because it's not entirely in my realm, which means it's not entirely in yours either. Maybe that whole particle—wave nonsense isn't so far off after all.

Energy that sometimes acts as if it has matter might be the best way for you to understand the soul.

Tad's soul was ... well, now I'm tangled up in the same net as you. I want to tell you what it looked like, the incredible colour it sang out when it left me and all my poor efforts behind, but that's another of your delightful paradoxes. Just as you can't comprehend anything you can't name, you can't name anything you haven't comprehended. You see so few of the colours that exist, I can't begin to tell you what he looked like. But I can tell you that, even to me, who typically doesn't have much time for such nonsense, he was a beautiful light.

But I'm getting ahead of myself. I should start with introductions. You can call me Ella. I admit I hijacked that name a long time ago just to irritate a former friend of mine, but I've since grown attached to it. You generally assign me a whole host of other preposterous monikers, when you deign to acknowledge me at all. But the one that most nearly approaches the truth is "Adversary", which has its own set of incorrect preconceptions. I'm not your adversary, specifically. That's just the part I play. You could just as easily name me "Juxtaposition". Whenever you come to a crossroads, I'm that perpendicular track. I'm the choice some of you find so necessary to the concept of free will; what others of you deny even exists in favour of behavioural predestination. I think the least imaginative name I've heard is "the devil", but I'll answer to it if I must. My bad rap comes from the fact that the choice I offer is always, unapologetically, carnal.

That's an old-fashioned word these days. Basically, it's fancy talk for me being far more committed to this creative experiment called the universe than any of the other players are. But don't be fooled. You were always designed with me in mind. Just because I'm the Adversary, doesn't make me your enemy. Although, my interest in your dilemmas is undeniably more dispassionate than the curious clowns on the other side.

Honestly, I'm not the bad guy here. If you want to assign dubious motives to anyone, you should start with the Creator who set this game in motion in the first place, who trapped your strange little wandering souls in flesh-cages and then demanded you look away from the material. I'm the one trying to persuade you to fully exist in the space you've been given, to enjoy every possible sensation to its *fullest. I'm here to remind you who you are, not who you could be. I'm about the immediate, the tangible, the tasty — the personal.*

After all, nothing fascinates you — or me — so much as identity. You're constantly figuring out who you are and laying claim to the name of the hour. You define whole periods of your life by these efforts and yet never seem to actually finish it. You're testing your boundaries as teenagers, you're indulging in mid-life crises a few decades later, and then there's the new and somehow undreamt-of tragedy of empty-nesting or retirement. And in all of these little dramas, you measure your successes and failures by the exchanges you have with the other people in your life. The Creator set you up with this notion that on some level, your life is about relationships. You gauge your own worth by how good a mother, a friend, a daughter, a worker you are.

I offer a different perspective. I want to know you for your own sake. I want a quiet moment, away from all those people with their needs and wants and demands and expectations, to hear what you want. What you need. What you expect and long for and ache without. If you give me the chance, I can offer you everything They tell you to sacrifice. I just need a moment alone with you.

I happen to have a gift for solitude. All it requires is a small hurt. Large hurts create their own loneliness, but in the right hands, even something as innocuous as an unready word can isolate. I'm always looking for these small hurts, these quiet quarantines of the soul I can craft into islands of the spirit. There I can persuade you of all the delightful comforts of the flesh. There I can tempt you onto an unfamiliar path. If alone weren't by far the better course, why would I have chosen it?

The board we're playing on, with all its coloured spaces, was laid out long ago. The game rarely requires much interference from me these days. Most people who face a choice between pleasure and sacrifice choose pleasure without prompting. For instance, I'd caution you to be highly sceptical of the hit-and-run driver who claims "the devil made me do it." As if he needed any persuading. But some dilemmas are delightfully complex. Sometimes I truly have no idea what you're about to do. And neither does that Maker of yours, no matter what anyone tells you about how They always have a plan. What silliness. Why would They bother with a game whose every move was predetermined? Your whole appeal to any of us lies in your unpredictability.

Which brings us back to Tad, and why he held my interest more than most.

If I took my job more seriously, I'd probably start tracking your tendencies at an earlier age, but it's so rarely worth the effort. Everyone knows that old saying about "give a teacher a child till she's seven years old, and he'll dictate her destiny", but nothing could be further from the truth. I could pop in for a brief altercation at age 15, age 25, age 45, and send you careening completely off track with hardly any effort at all. Sure, you would feel conflicted about your new place in the cornfield, but your feelings are no concern of mine. Just your choices. And those are rarely difficult to affect.

Tad was different. I'm going to have to try and find a way to describe his light to you, a way that doesn't rely on colours or hues or intensities. It's contrary to what I generally work to accomplish, but bear with me for just a minute. Close your eyes and imagine a star so distant, so far away in time, that its light that burned out a million years ago still hasn't reached the earth. But it's coming. It's travelling, undeterred by the absence of its origin. Now imagine the moment that light finally arrives, how its shaft falls thousands of feet through the ocean and illuminates every secret on its way through. Imagine how it strikes the ocean floor, finds the fellow of its birthplace, and absorbs that dark light emitted by the earth itself. The gloaming brilliance refracted in that moment — that's what I felt when I first encountered Tad.

His light remained as brilliant and singular and ancient at the conclusion of his journey as it had been at the beginning. So utterly itself.

I can see that doesn't help you. Which is good news for me. The less you understand of what you can't see, the better. Part of the lovely fallout of the whole "creation science" movement is how increasingly impossible it makes any faith in the unseen, even among those who claim to live by faith. And if I'm going to keep coming out on top, I need to keep you firmly in the realm of the felt. The mind that balks at quantum particles definitely won't be able to accept the folderol of a soul. Oh sure, you can spout a limited number of mass-produced slogans that pretend at spirituality, but it's not the sort of thing that will stand up to a real defence.

I guess I'll just show you. This story will make the most sense if I let you see the world through his mother's eyes, since her crossroads are the ones I'm arguing counted the most. As far as narrative goes, anyway — she writes the beginning and chooses the end. Which is funny when you think about it: one of the prevailing misconceptions of humanity is the all-consuming importance of every decision you make. You really took that whole butterfly theory to heart. Somehow you are utterly convinced that every step you take dictates the course of the universe. This self-absorption plays well to my purposes. Your conviction of your own importance produces anxiety, shame, guilt, fear, even pride — all emotions that leave you aching for some relief. And relief is what I offer in spades. I am the one who soothes, who comforts, who feeds.

But in this case, I grant Perdie the reality she perceives: that her choices, to go or to stay, dictate what will become of those she loves most. It's the sort of dilemma I live for. High risk on every side, with no way to know for sure what you'll choose. She should have fascinated me, but I was distracted by Tad along the way.

Tad was the strangest compound of self-contained and unselfish, elements unfamiliar to most of you and intriguing to me. I necessarily draw all my own definition and purpose from my *intersections with you. Sometimes I think you poor paltry mortals hold all the power in this game, objects of curiosity and longing toward whom all heaven is bent.*

In the story I have to tell, Tad keeps his own path undeterred by how often his steps cross mine. He doesn't even acknowledge me, and that, as much as anything, enchants me.

Perdie, though, is continually engaged in my world, doubting every decision she makes, imagining her every act the crux of some new destiny. So I'll give her the place of storyteller here. You'll have to tell me by the end if she reminds you of anyone you know.

BEFORE THE ACCIDENT

CHAPTER ONE

"You know this is the only way," Perdie sighed, scraping back the strands of brown hair that had fallen loose from her ponytail.

"Are you sure?" Julie asked, her brow furrowed as she absently shook a doll in the direction of her three-year-old daughter. Lexie ran over and grabbed the rag-haired toy with a high-pitched squeal that barely registered to either mother. Julie frowned more deeply; her attention no longer divided. "What if he comes after you? Or charges you with kidnapping?"

"I'm not saying it's not a gamble. It is. But it's the only chance I have. And I think I at least have a fair chance of neither of those things happening. Matt's … very particular. He won't leave his classes mid-term. And he won't have me charged." Perdie's gaze drifted, darkened. "He can't admit to that kind of loss of control. At least, that's what I'm banking on."

"I hope you're right … But how will you survive out there? Isn't Colorado an expensive place to live?"

Perdie's eyes rested on her youngest child. Tad was just a year older than Lexie, but Perdie couldn't help noticing that their play was much more parallel than cooperative. He didn't ignore his younger playmate, exactly. It was more as if he humoured her, giving her just enough attention so that she would allow him to focus on his real interest: building a complex series of walls and towers out of alphabet blocks. It struck her as oddly self-aware for a four-year-old. Neither of her older girls had demonstrated that level of social acuity so young. In fact, she didn't think they possessed it now, at ages seven and ten.

With an effort, Perdie dragged her focus back to her troubled friend. It wasn't that she didn't want to reassure Julie, or that she doubted her good intentions; it was that she'd been over this a thousand times in her head, lying awake in the dark in a too-warm bed. Repeating aloud every argument she'd already had with herself felt unutterably exhausting. But Julie's questions came from love, so Perdie forced herself to explain. "It is. But it's also over a thousand miles away from Ohio. Going east is even more expensive than going west, and too close. If I go as far south, I'm looking at higher crime rates and depressed economies. Colorado is expensive, but I think it's safer, and there's more work out there. At least, I hope so."

"Do you have any leads on jobs?"

Perdie shook her head. "Maybe if I'd gone to school, like you, and had a degree, I could get someone to take me seriously from across the country. But I haven't even gotten a call back on any of the resumes I've sent out. I don't think retail and office jobs have to hunt for applicants, and that's all I'm qualified for. I just have to hope that my little nest egg holds out till I find something we can live on."

"That sounds terrifying, Perdie. What if it doesn't?"

Perdie fixed her with a stare. "What if the next time Matt

loses his temper my kids end up motherless? I'd rather wind up on government assistance than dead."

Colour rose to Julie's cheeks. "I'm sorry. I didn't mean — I just want to be sure you've thought this through. That you're in as good a position as you can be. Are you sure it wouldn't help to go to the church, ask the leaders for help?"

"Maybe if the leaders were people like you, who would actually take some kind of action, I could consider that. But it's not like they'd help us get out. They'd just pray over us and tell Matt to ask for patience and understanding for his rebellious wife. Not to mention that Matt would kill me if I humiliated him by going outside the family. If he so much as guessed I'd ever told you about any of our fights, he'd break every rib in my body. He'd be beyond furious."

Julie pursed her lips. "I wish I could tell you that you're wrong. You do know Darren and I will do anything we can, though, don't you? If you get into trouble out there, if it takes a while to find a job, you have to promise to let us know. Darren's as sick about this as I am. We don't have much, but we would never let you starve."

Perdie barked out a short laugh in spite of herself. "I don't think we would starve. I've never navigated the welfare system, but I think the whole point is to keep people from starving. Childcare is my more pressing issue. Hannah's not quite old enough to be left alone with Rachel and Tad."

Perdie realised too late that Lexie had become completely engrossed in the cartoon playing on the television screen, leaving Tad's attention undivided. He was slowly and absently setting one block on top of another, clearly intent on listening to his mother's words. With a grimace, she gestured toward her son.

"Oh, crumbs," Julie muttered hastily.

"Who wants Kool-Aid?" Perdie asked with determined cheerfulness, clapping her hands and rising to her feet.

"I do, I do!" Lexie exclaimed, without shifting her gaze from the screen.

"Me, too," said Tad solemnly, watching his mother as she headed into the kitchen.

The subject was dropped, the rest of the conversation between the two women conveyed in silent looks and a too-tight hug as the playdate ended.

Later that night, as Perdie lay in that warm bed and felt her husband's rumbling snores reverberate through her body, she thought of her son's sombre gaze and wondered what lay behind those ageless eyes that had already seen too much.

CHAPTER TWO

Perdie's insides were shaking so violently she thought she might throw up. It was impossible to tell how much of her reaction was simple fear and how much was physical overexertion. Matt had left for a full day of classes at 6:30 that morning, but there was never any guarantee he wouldn't stop home for lunch on a whim. Not that there was anything remotely whimsical or sweet about his drive to continually check up on her. Today had been a lucky day, though. She'd fielded two calls and a text message, but he'd stayed on campus for lunch. No doubt taking the opportunity to wow some besotted student with his insights. Perdie knew she should be concerned for the next woman to fall into his trap, but she could only summon up gratitude for anything that diverted his focus away from her.

She'd made her peace months ago, back when she first hatched up this plan, with all the belongings she'd be leaving behind. There wouldn't be time to pack, and she couldn't afford a big trailer anyway. Resolutely, she kept her gaze from lingering on the massive, old oak table Aunt Lorna had given her as a wedding gift. How many family holidays had she spent as a kid, crowded around its battered surface teeming with overflowing platters and kid-crafted place settings? When she'd first married Matt and dutifully joined his church, she'd dreamed of playdates and dinner parties, imagined their growing family a hub of hospitality and happiness. That had been the worst sort of folly, of course. Now she kept every imperfection on the scarred wood carefully hidden away beneath a lace tablecloth. Matt had only consented to let her keep it because it was solid wood, a pricey indulgence for a young couple.

For one moment, she pushed aside her terrified urgency and slid her hand beneath the lace. Against her palm, she felt the scratches of heavy dinner plates and childish pens, the rough reassurance of old varnish. Warmth seemed to emanate up her arm, the living flame of every woman who had ever set a plate or rested her weary head on that table. Her heartstrings threatened to tear when she pictured Matt sitting alone at this table in an empty house, never knowing its true worth, but they stubbornly stitched themselves back up.

Seems like a perfect moment for me to intrude, doesn't it? Flood Perdie's mouth with the acrid flavour of bitterness, consume her mind with regrets and losses disguised as nostalgia. For most people, you'd be right. But this wasn't an intersection Perdie even acknowledged. Perdie's dilemma would require more sophistication than the blunt instrument of selfishness. She makes this sacrifice look positively easy...

So she had to leave the table behind. With it, she'd leave every memory of cold, tense, silent suppers. Even as a talisman of familial love, this table hadn't served a single meal to nourish the heart while Matt sat at its head. She'd build a new happiness for her kids, even if they had to eat pizza off paper plates, sitting on an apartment floor.

She pulled her hand away, squared her shoulders.

Her only priority was the kids' stuff. It was going to be hard enough for them to start over in a new place surrounded by strangers. She was determined they would at least be able to close their eyes at night and pretend they felt at home.

She'd filled the inflatable pool first thing this morning and stuck the kids in the backyard. Snacks and drinks on the back porch meant they shouldn't have any reason to come indoors and catch her hauling all their furniture and armfuls of clothes into the mini U-Haul trailer Darren and Julie had dropped off for her earlier this morning. They'd both offered to stay and help her pack it up, but Perdie was adamant in her refusal. It was still possible that Matt would come home and catch her. Darren and Julie's presence would only guarantee the worst possible outcome. Losing face was a possibility no narcissist could permit. Given enough time and distance, Matt might eventually accept her defection, but he'd never allow himself to be humiliated. A key element of her escape was allowing him to write the story after she left. He could play the victim all he wanted once she was gone — cast her as the cruel, selfish woman who'd stolen his children and run away without so much as a goodbye.

It had taken some convincing, but she'd known the price of backing down would be too high to pay. She'd let this go on for too long as it was. Adding more victims to the fallout wasn't an option. This was her mess, and she was cleaning it up. Not to mention she still had the niggling, persistent fear that Matt would cry and plead and convince Darren and Julie that she was the villain after all. She'd watched him manipulate too many people too deftly to discount him, even among those she counted as friends.

Of course, she'd known her plan wouldn't long survive contact with the enemy, by which she meant her own kids. Tad would happily stay in the pool till his skin permanently raisined, but Hannah and Rachel — mostly Hannah — soon bored of waterplay and kept trying to come in. She'd locked the back door, which just meant that Hannah came wandering around the front of the house to get in and caught her mom staggering toward the trailer with two tubs of toys.

"Mom! What's happening? Where are we going?"

By this point, Perdie was already too tired and too afraid to react much to being caught out by her ten-year-old daughter. She'd simply shoved her brown hair out of her eyes and panted out, "We're going on a trip. But it's a surprise. Help me keep your sister and brother out of the front yard till we're ready to go."

Perdie wasn't any more or less perceptive a mother than any other, but even in her own distress, she caught it: the instant her daughter's soul snapped shut, a nearly invisible locking-down that was nothing more than a flicker in her brown eyes — the only genetic nod to her mother's input in a face that otherwise mirrored her father's handsome Nordic influence.

Perdie didn't know what to do about it, of course, but she did see it. Saw it, and grieved it. Ten years was just too long to have seen such violence, even if it stayed mostly behind closed doors. And leaving meant the end of the fairy tales and lies children inevitably spin to make sense of their own horrors: Hannah's father was not suffering under an evil enchantment, her mother was not going to rescue them all, they were not going to live happily ever after.

Her father was a bad man, her mother was giving up, and they were running away. So, standing there in the hot Ohio sun in a cookie-cutter suburban neighbourhood, hope died on the driveway, and Hannah grew up.

"Okay. Where are we going?"

"Colorado. To the mountains."

Hannah's face brightened at that. Cornfield kids can't help but be cheered by the thought of mountains, even in the darkest of circumstances.

"Can I grab a book? I'll stay in the backyard. I'm just tired of the pool."

Perdie hadn't gotten to the bookshelves yet. Between the kids' beds and dressers, she wouldn't have room for shelves, but she intended to take as many armfuls of books as she could all the same. She hardly had time to read herself, but all three of the kids were voracious, even Tad.

"Go for it. Just — keep track of it, okay? Or it might get left behind."

Perdie wanted to be surprised that Hannah hadn't asked why they were taking mattresses and dresser drawers on vacation, but she knew that Hannah had grasped the situation more swiftly than a ten-year-old girl should be able to. If Hannah was willing to pretend to swallow her mom's story for the time being, then Perdie was going to let her and be grateful.

She stuffed her clothes, hangers and all, on top and around the corners of the kids' stuff. She stacked the photo albums in with the books. She'd planned ahead, of course — planned for months — so she had a stash of paper plates, napkins, and plastic glasses and tableware. She took a saucepan and a skillet and a couple large utensils, but that was it. She didn't intend to give Matt any ammunition to use against her. She even left all the photos on the walls, her Colonial-themed décor and baskets. She did squeeze in all the throw pillows, though. Matt found the things frippery and pointless, and they'd be glad of something to sit on when they got to their new apartment, even if it was just a pillow on the floor.

Between Hannah helping keep Rachel and Tad corralled, and Perdie's own ruthless abandonment of virtually every personal possession, she managed to get the trailer packed up by 2:30. That gave her two hours before Matt made it home and discovered they were gone. Not much of a head start, but then, she wasn't expecting him to chase after them, either. He had classes tomorrow, too, and there was no way Matt Blevins would admit that he'd lost so much control over his household that he had to cancel classes to chase down his wife.

There had been a time when his narcissistic tendencies had terrified her, but in time, she'd learned to bend them to her own purposes. With mixed results, but still. She had to take back some semblance of power in her own life. And if that made her as much of a manipulator as he, so be it. She'd accepted her role as victim for far too long. If getting out from under those fists made her a villain, too, she wasn't about to lose any sleep over it.

She ran through the house one last time, forcing her eyes to focus with immense effort. She was already so exhausted, as much from the constant terror of Matt coming home early as the difficulties of dragging out the furniture. Part of her still didn't accept this was actually happening. She'd been expecting to die for so long now, it seemed preposterous to expect that she might live, after all.

On an impulse, she scooped up one last item: a delicately carved little soap dish that looked like a birds' nest with a robin perched on its edge. It had been a gift from Julie. *This is mine*, she thought fiercely. *I'm keeping it.*

Now for the hard part. Getting the kids into the minivan would be easy. They were always up for an adventure, and even a trip to the library qualified. Telling them they were never coming back: that was going to be something else entirely.

The one thing I'll grant you about Perdie is that she was fierce. That might seem oxymoronic — a fierce, battered wife? But they're more common than you think. She'd had her reasons for staying, and she knew what they were. Now that she'd been given a bigger reason for leaving, nothing was going to deter her from that path, certainly not her own fear and inadequacy. One of my favourite things about you humans is how willingly you will run pell-mell into situations you are entirely unequipped to handle. As often as not, you even prevail through sheer obstinacy. Perdie was one of those sorts. She didn't know the healthy way to break the news to her kids that they were moving over a thousand miles away and, for all intents and purposes, didn't have a daddy anymore; but she was bound and determined to do it anyway.

CHAPTER THREE

I've always been amused, both by the fact that Jesus had the gall to say it and by how earnestly so many of you took him when he did. "Be anxious in nothing." Seriously? Anxiety is the fundamental definition of the human condition. You pathetic creatures can't count on anything, least of all the most basic of things, which is simple existence.

You don't even know if you'll be breathing one minute to the next, and you're supposed to eschew anxiety? You are the only reason anxiety is a concept. In fact, you could say it's the source of your occasional nobility. After all, most of us rest pretty easy in our persistence. We at least know that we're not going to blink out because we trip and fall, or because we fail to effectively ingest dead things through our system in a regular fashion, or because one bodily system or another simply ceases. Or hiccups. A mere hiccup in one of your many organs, and out you go like a light.

And that's assuming a benevolent world. We can't forget that many of you devote most of your wretched hours solely to making everyone around you miserable. Not on purpose, I mean (besides the obvious exception of the actual psychopaths). Making people miserable on purpose would require some principle and dedication. No, it's just a level of selfishness so extreme that it wreaks havoc on everyone it touches.

I know what you're thinking — that that's my fault, right? That I must just delight in the refuse that parades around in human skin? But that's where you're wrong. Mostly wrong, anyway.

Remember, I'm the Adversary. All my power, my pleasure, comes from my opposition to your ends. And I do make no apology for the fact that I am relentlessly immediate, sensual, material in my intentions. Anyway, back to the anxiety thing. I'll never know why you take some of the crazy stuff Jesus spouted at face value and assign others high existential symbolism. Clearly, he was being a little facetious. I mean, he set this whole system up so that anxiety is the grease that keeps the gears running. You usually refer to it as "survival instincts", but it's the same thing. Where it becomes most useful to me is in its redundancies. Some of you operate like machines that can't be shut down. One process completes, and another immediately begins. Modern society accommodates this so beautifully, with its endless expectations of recreation and relaxation and self-care.

Which is where I should shine, but you so often manage to ruin even that for me. You scrimp and save and work toward some goal — a spa day, a cruise, even just a weekend with the family. Invariably you spend at least half of the time that ought to be consumed with pleasure and sensation dreading the return to work, the arrival of the bill. The benefit to me is that the angst-riddled person is most likely to seize on whatever next delight I proffer. Still, the cycle is exhausting. I'd love for you to choose my path for its own sake and actually breathe the air there for a moment. The beauties of this world are already so terribly brief, and you shorten them even more with your incessant dissatisfaction. It's a quality neither I nor your Creator much enjoy.

But who knows to what extent this anxiety contributes to your lovely inconstancy, your stumbling fickleness? Perhaps it's more than survival. Perhaps it's poetry, of a sort. Every time I think I have you fast in my palm, you throw all my gifts away and choose what cannot be seen or held.

At the time of your inception, I think you were mostly just an intellectual exercise, a sort of philosophical curiosity, and still, you — these creatures who insisted on pursuing idealistic impossibilities as if they weren't mortal at all — turned out to be the most fascinating beings any of us have ever encountered. That's the whole appeal of humanity.

And ascetics and atheists and stoics and misanthropes notwithstanding, most of you know this at bottom. That's why stories like the 300 of Sparta have such lasting significance. The insane notion that, in the face of unavoidable defeat, there is still virtue in a battle well fought, is simply delightful. Such beautiful, hopeless striving after all that is antagonistic to your very being. It does make some sense for the few of you who actually still do believe in a reality apart from the physical world, but this crazy virtue isn't limited to reason. Plenty of atheists who are absolutely determined that the body is no husk but the world entire, nonetheless give their lives over to the truly fanciful impulse to practice kindness or improve conditions. Why?

For me — for all the Others, really — that's when you become interesting. Contrary to what the Sunday school teachers may tell you, I have no interest at all in those of you who are swallowed up in selfishness. I live in the tension, in the dilemma, in the crossroads. The meth-head and the murderer are, for the most part, as boring to me as they are intriguing to you. Known quantities. But give me an addict considering rehab or a woman torn between killing her husband in his sleep and running away, and now you've piqued my interest.

And come on — be anxious for nothing? From the guy who could

*turn a few loaves and fishes into a feast for thousands? Come. On.
How seriously are we supposed to take that?*

CHAPTER FOUR

Perdie focused on what she could control. She kept her hands loosely wrapped around the steering wheel, kept her shoulders back, kept her eyes forward. She kept her voice modulated and soft. There was so much she couldn't control.

Hannah was the quietest.

Rachel was the saddest.

Tad was the angriest.

Explaining to her children that this trip had no road for return had been as awful as she had feared.

"I don't want to go!" Tad wailed, kicking his legs against the car seat. Hannah, the only one tall enough to ride shotgun, had turned her entire body to the passenger window, her fist curled under her chin. Her back was rigid, and Perdie had no idea what Hannah was seeing as she gazed out over the spring-ready cornfields. Rachel had calmed down for the moment, but her sniffles still punctuated the air.

"I promise," Tad said earnestly, and his voice dropped into such a mature cadence that Perdie was startled into meeting his eyes in the rear-view mirror. Dark eyes bright with tears, he speared her with a look so desperate in its longing that Perdie almost turned the car around.

"Mommy, I promise. I promise I'll be good. I promise."

Tad knew, Perdie thought with shock. He knew that he was the one she truly feared for. Matt wasn't some out-of-control animal, after all. Once Perdie had learned the rules, the expectations of her marriage, she'd become pretty good at keeping the violence at a minimum. That was her job, she knew. Managing her husband's temper and his reactions was her responsibility, and she'd always shouldered the blame when she'd mis-stepped.

There were still the nights when Matt came home in a fury over something she'd had nothing to do with, and all her soothing efforts backfired. There was no way of avoiding that. The one thing she'd always been able to count on, though, was that his anger was limited to her. He treated his daughters like princesses.

And for a while, that grace had extended to Tad. At first, Matt had been so delighted, so enchanted with his son. He'd adored everything about the sombre, quiet little baby who watched and listened and learned all the time. He'd never tired of toting him around and showing him off. But as Tad had grown from a baby into a little boy — whose quiet, watchful eyes saw and silently condemned, who calmly and deliberately did exactly what he'd been told not to, who said no without shame or compunction — Matt's regard changed. What he'd found cute and mildly troublesome in his daughters, he found inexcusably rebellious in his son. Naughtiness in a three-year-old daughter was hatefulness in a three-year-old son. Matt expected — he needed — complete adoration and slavish obedience. A son, a would-be man who might oppose him, could not be tolerated.

Perdie had nearly missed the danger signs at first. It began as a sharper edge of irritation than warranted, a shortness of tone, a bare sliver of rage beneath the surface. An impatience with the sleepy, evening-time crankiness of the two-year-old, a flash of temper at the upstart of the three-year-old. Matt had never spanked the girls, favouring timeouts and stern looks over physical punishment. But he was quick to swat Tad or smack his hand — actions that startled Perdie and caught her notice at last, if only for how unexpected the impulse seemed where the kids were concerned. Foolishly, she'd still thought her body would be as sufficient a buffer for Tad as it had been for Rachel and Hannah. Perdie had long ago lost track of how many times Matt had wept in exasperated fury after he'd taken out his frustration with her lax parenting skills and the children's spoiled natures on her. She took an odd comfort in the fact that Matt never struck her where it would leave unconcealable marks. It promised what she suspected, what she hoped: that Matt's anger was not truly out of control. After all, even with great provocation, he'd never lost his temper and hit her in public or left her face bloodied. She didn't have to worry about him flying off the handle and hurting her worse than he intended. Perdie knew it wasn't healthy to find reassurance in the fully deliberate nature of her husband's cruelty; but then, she'd given up on healthy a long time ago.

The turning point had come seven months before. Six-year-old Rachel had been desperately ill. Cold medicine hadn't done the trick, and Perdie and Matt had bundled the kids into the car for a late-night emergency room trip. Matt had driven, and Perdie had crouched in the centre row of the minivan, anxiously watching Rachel's laboured breathing, her cell phone in her hand, just in case she needed to call 911.

Double pneumonia had been the diagnosis. Matt had sat in the waiting room with nine-year-old Hannah and three-year-old Tad. Hannah had brought her hardbound copy of something about dragons and spent the two-hour wait curled up in the corner of a plastic chair, all attention focused inward. It had been up to Matt to occupy the toddler they'd roused from sleep and drug down to the fluorescent-lit, glaringly sterile hospital lobby with only the couple of toys that had been stuffed into Perdie's purse the last time they went to church.

Perdie had known that it would be trying for Matt, of course. He was rarely — make that never — solely responsible for childcare. Even when she went to the grocery store, Perdie always took at least the two youngest, if not all three children. Matt's duties as father were all window-dressing. But she'd been so worried about Rachel, so focused on that terrible sawing sound rattling from her daughter's chest, that she'd left the other two with their father without a second thought.

She'd realised her mistake the moment she'd stepped back into the waiting room with a sleeping Rachel in her aching arms and a handful of prescriptions clutched in her sweaty palm. Matt's eyes had blazed at her across the strangers crowded into the late-night lobby in varying stages of distress. In his blue gaze, she'd read sheer hatred and boundless resentment. Now that her worry over her youngest daughter had been eased, she grasped the new danger in an instant.

Wrangling an inconsolably fussy little boy in a roomful of people, where his struggle featured as the only entertainment aside from the Fox News ticker tape scrolling across a dingy corner television, had left Matt feeling like a fool, and there was no emotion more hazardous for Perdie than her husband's humiliation. She should have known better. She should have taken Tad with her. It was too late to remedy that now, of course. She set her jaw, straightened her spine against Rachel's warm weight, damp with sleepy-child sweat and fever, straightened her shoulder against the consequence she knew she would have to pay once they got home, and met his gaze with as much regret and remorse as she could muster.

"Get up, Hannah," Matt had ordered tersely.

"Just a sec," she'd mumbled, too absorbed in her reading to register the warning signs she'd long ago learned to identify.

"Now, Hannah!" Matt's voice had crackled across the waiting room like a flash of lightning. Hannah had jumped hard, snapping her book shut without saving her place and shooting her mother a look pathetic in its apology. They both knew it was too little, too late, but Perdie didn't blame her daughter. She was just a tired little girl who'd been pulled out of her bed in the middle of the night. Hannah had long ago taken on the role of the good child, mimicking her mother's efforts to keep things smooth and deflect the violence that always threatened just below the surface. Perdie knew it wasn't right for a little girl to feel responsible for whether or not her mother got hit, but she hadn't known how to counter the impulse. Especially when it resulted in exactly the behaviour she needed to survive.

Hannah slipped her sock-clad feet back into her sandals and came to attention, falling in silently behind her parents as Perdie bent her knees to awkwardly grab Tad's blanket off the back of a chair without disturbing Rachel.

"Come on, Tad," his mother wheedled hopefully. "We have to leave the blocks here. We can finally go home. I'll make you a warm glass of milk when we get there."

Warm milk with sugar and cinnamon was a favourite bedtime treat for all three children, but Tad didn't look up. His dark-hollowed eyes and chubby fingers were intent on their task.

That's when it happened.

Matt's simmering rage boiled over. His hand flew so fast,

Perdie barely had time to register it. She knew if that blow made contact, it would send her son flying across the lobby.

A scream strangled in her throat, though no sound emitted from her parted lips. Without thinking, she stepped between her husband and son, Matt's backhand thudding against her spine.

"Tad," she gasped out. "Come with Mommy. Now. It's time to go home."

Other than a few swiftly downcast stares and couple of irritated harrumphs from two white-haired ladies, no one paid mind to their little family tableau. But as much as she wished otherwise, Tad had clearly realised his error. The moment his father's raging energy had turned in his direction, the toddler had frozen, lashes resting on pale cheeks, fist clutching a red block suspended in air. At Perdie's harshly whispered "Now", he came back to life, scrambling up and running to latch himself on to his mother's leg farthest from his father. Hannah slipped around them, face burning, walking toward the exit as quickly as she could.

The instant his knuckles had touched Perdie, Matt had pulled himself fiercely back under control. His smarting gaze promised retribution as she swung back around, one hand resting protectively on Tad's head, the other under Rachel's bottom as she pushed up the six-year-old higher on her shoulder. For the first time in a long time, Perdie hadn't bothered to regulate her own expression as she met her husband's eyes. She'd positively seared him, fury and hatred blazing defiantly.

After all the months and years of me trying to alert Perdie to the crossroads where she stood, she'd finally perceived that there was more than one route away from this convergence. She set the first step on the road that led away from her husband in that moment, when she revealed to him, without a word, without holding back, without caution, how desperately she wanted him dead.

Another man might have been pricked by that knowledge. Might have been hurt. Might have even been frightened. But for Matt, whose wife and children existed solely as an extension of his own identity, it was an unconscionable rebellion. And likewise, without a word, without caution, he told her, absolutely, that she and their children would die long before he would. That every breath they took had been gifted by him, only him, and he would readily take that gift back if he chose.

Of course, no one but me saw all that.

That night, after she'd tucked the children back into their beds, Perdie had endured her husband's fists and fury with a calm that terrified even herself. That was the night she'd realised she couldn't protect her children any longer. Matt had stepped too far by aiming for Tad, and it was possible that, having once crossed that line, he'd start taking out his fury on the girls as well. Regardless, Perdie could no longer rely on the one truth that she'd clung to in her decision to stay: the notion her children were in no danger from their father.

She felt like an elephant seal cow, unwieldy, slow, out of her element on the shore, desperate to hide her calves from the violent bull bearing down on them, compelled to fight but fatalistic in the acceptance of their certain end.

So today, in the car, when four-year-old Tad promised so dearly, so earnestly, to be good, she knew what he meant. More than anything, she wished he didn't feel that he needed to be good to be loved. She could only hope he was too little to keep this memory fast. Rachel and Hannah wouldn't have that grace, she knew.

Still, she tried. She trotted out all the tired old clichés she could.

"Oh, Tad. This isn't your fault. It's none of your faults. Not you, Rachel, and not you, Hannah. Sometimes mommies just have to do the right thing, no matter how hard it is. This is one of those times. None of you did anything to make this happen."

The words sounded hollow falling from her lips, striking the floor of the minivan, bouncing tiredly before rolling out of reach under the seats. Perdie kept her eyes on the road, unable to again face the grief and loss shining in her children's faces.

"What about my friends?" Rachel protested. "What about school?"

By a huge stroke of luck, the school system had long ago opted to offset their fall break with the college. That meant that Matt had been off last week, and the kids were off this week. Perdie had no idea how she'd have managed to pull off their escape otherwise.

"I've been in touch with the schools in Colorado. You girls are both already enrolled. You won't miss a beat."

"Just all of our friends," Hannah muttered, barely loud enough for Perdie to hear. Her chest ached.

"Look, I'm not going to pretend there isn't a downside to this. There is. A lot of things are going to be harder. I'm going to need each of you to help in ways maybe you haven't helped before. We're all going to have to pull together to get through this. And most of all, I need you to do this one thing for me." Perdie drew a deep breath, rewrapped her fingers on the steering wheel. "I'm asking you to believe that I have made this decision solely because I truly think it's what's best for you. It's my job as your mom to look out for you. There are things you don't know — things you can't understand just yet, but, I swear to you, this is the best thing for all of us. The only thing."

"Best for you, maybe." Rachel threw the words at her

mother from the back seat. "We're not the ones who make Daddy mad. You are. This is your fault."

Bile rose in Perdie's throat, but she swallowed it and forced herself to go on. "I know it seems that way."

This was her fault, she thought, but not in the way Rachel meant. It was her fault that her children believed, without question, what she had never told them in words but had demonstrated every day she stayed: that abuse was the fault of the victim, that fear and pain were the price of being flawed. It was her fault she'd stayed so long that they'd grown inured to terror the only way they knew how: by sympathising with the aggressor. It was her fault that she'd chosen a monster as a partner in her life.

There was no way to explain her rationale: that as long as she was the only one collecting bruises and bloody rags, she'd thought it a fair price for staying home with her children, cooking a real supper for them every night, scheduling play-dates, spending days at the park or at the museum. She hadn't wanted her sweet babies to become latchkey kids, to hesitate to call their mom when they were scared or sick because she was busy at work, to feel the void of safety and security that a doting father provided. She'd thought — no, she'd known — she could be a better mom if she had the luxury of staying home and being only that, rather than trying to juggle working hours and childcare and teacher phone calls and runny noses.

It wasn't Tad's fault that he was born a boy. It wasn't his fault that he saw the cruelty in his father. It wasn't his fault he threatened his father's manhood simply by existing. But it was her job to make sure he never paid the consequence of those truths.

And that was more than she could say. Better her children

hate her than have to bear up under the truth she carried in her broken bones.

"It's okay if you're angry. But this is happening whether you're angry or not. And whether or not you're angry, we are still a family, and we will still get through this together."

"And Daddy?" Rachel flung back at her. "Isn't Daddy part of our family?"

"Your daddy had a choice of his own to make, and he didn't choose us," Perdie told her middle child flatly. "But I am choosing you. I am choosing you above everything. We're going to build a new life, and it's going to be beautiful."

CHAPTER FIVE

Perdie had the best of intentions, but intentions don't take anyone very far. Any apartment in Fort Collins, Colorado was expensive, but a three bedroom was truly outrageous. She'd had a plan, though. Between the prices and the housing shortage, she'd counted on finding a college student willing to live rent-free in the apartment in exchange for babysitting. She'd had enough money saved to pay the first six-month lease outright, which gave her a little breathing room.

She even found a perfectly suitable candidate less than two weeks after moving in. Jessa was a mechanical engineering student, quiet, kind, and not any messier than Rachel, which was just this side of tolerable. Perdie was out pounding the streets every spare minute she could, dropping off her resume at doctors' offices, hair salons, and department stores. Within a month, she had a full-time management position with one of the mall department stores. She volunteered for as many closing shifts as possible so she didn't overlap with Jessa's classes.

The problem, of course, was money.

Perdie didn't understand how anyone could survive financially in this town. She would need at least two, maybe three, jobs at her current pay rate to continue living in this apartment. They could downsize, but she was already sleeping on a futon in the living room so Jessa had a room of her own. Not to mention that having Hannah and Rachel in the same tiny room hadn't been a stunning parenting success in its own right. Hannah would just brood until Rachel's messiness crossed some invisible line in her head, and then she'd blow like Krakatoa.

A smaller apartment would mean losing their childcare option, and even just a few hours before and after school was pricey for three children, and Tad wasn't in school yet, and summer was coming, which meant skyrocketing costs. The only reason they appeared to be remaining afloat now was because of that prepayment on the rent. With the college campus nearby, Fort Collins was swamped with over-qualified workers for even the most menial positions. BA's filled fast food counters, and Master's students brewed coffee. Perdie had married Matt right out of high school and had never gone to school again. It was something of a miracle she'd managed to score the management position in a department store.

As for her promise of a beautiful life — she guessed it depended on how you gauged that. She couldn't blame the kids for not seeing it at all. She was actually sleeping through the night for the first time in she didn't know how long. The absence of fear — and what had been even more insidious: that constant, never-relenting anxiety that frothed and roiled beneath every decision she made, from how she folded the clothes to what she made for dinner, to how loud the TV volume was when she turned it on — was exhilarating. She felt ten years younger. She felt strong, powerful, capable, words she'd never considered in relation to herself before.

She delighted in the small things — leaving the dirty dishes on the counter before she went to bed at night, opening the windows early in the morning to listen to the birds sing, ignoring the clean laundry waiting to be folded in the dryer. She bought three different kinds of Pop-Tarts. She and the kids had popcorn nights in front of the TV, and the sight of a few kernels on the carpet didn't strike her stomach with a punch of fear. They went for bike rides on the city trails and played at the park, and she didn't shush the children and rush them into the showers as soon as they came back inside.

But perhaps Perdie had done too good a job of protecting the children from their father's rage, because their perception of gain versus loss was very different from hers. Sure, their home was more peaceful, their mom happier, their belongings more joyfully haphazard. But they'd lost their big backyard, their bedrooms, their friends, their father. They knew, of course. No amount of sheltering could keep them completely ignorant of that level of violence. But it had never truly turned on them. Matt had doted on his daughters, indulged them, spoiled them, holding only Perdie accountable for any of their failings. Even Tad had been exempt from his father's ire for most of his life. Perdie knew what it was to see murder in a man's eyes. Her children did not. How could they conceive of a reality where their own father might end their lives?

So she told herself it was hardly surprising they resented her for not being good enough to stay. For pushing what must be a generous and loving man into violence that he despised in himself. She tried to absorb Rachel and Hannah's fulminating looks and cold shoulders as a normal part of the process of a family disbanding. She told herself that she was more than willing to be the bad guy if it meant giving her children a safe and healthy home.

But it still hurt. God, did it hurt.

Surprisingly, Tad was most forgiving of the three. Perhaps that wasn't so surprising after all. As the only child not in school, he'd lost fewer relationships as a consequence of the move. His mom was still very much his best friend. And while the girls had still enjoyed their favoured status in their dad's affections, Tad had become the problem child, frequently earning his father's exasperation and recrimination. Perdie knew that Matt's slip in the hospital had made an indelible impression on Tad. So maybe it wasn't surprising in the least that Tad adjusted to their new lives most easily.

What was hardest for Perdie wasn't the new worry of whether or not she would be able to pay the bills, or the juggling of schedules, or the loneliness, or even the bitterly hostile exchanges between Matt and the divorce attorneys. The hardest thing was how little time she had with her children. Back in Ohio, she'd fixed her children breakfast every morning and tucked them into bed at night. Her days were filled with chores and cooking and playdates and trips to the park. If Rachel forgot her lunchbox, Perdie just ran it over to the school for her. If Hannah was sick, Perdie picked her up. If Tad was feeling fussy, Perdie bundled him up, and they spent the day at the park or on the trails together. If the teacher needed volunteers for a field trip or a class party, Perdie was first on the list.

Shift work at the department store meant Perdie might not see her kids one evening and then have to go to work again the next morning before they woke up. If they forgot their lunch or their homework, odds were there was nothing she could do to help. What few hours they did spend together were task-oriented — finishing homework, taking baths, cleaning rooms — all while Perdie scrambled to prep meals and make lunches and do laundry while she could. She didn't just miss her children — she missed the mom she used to be.

. . .

Her lowest point came three months after the move. She'd said good night to Rachel and Hannah in the (slightly) larger master bedroom that they shared. It was too early for them to go to sleep, but baths had been taken, homework was either done or lied about, and phones had been confiscated. When she'd left their room, they'd both been propped up in bed surrounded by pillows, noses deep in their books.

Thank goodness Tad hadn't outgrown being read to. Perdie wasn't ready to let go that last vestige of the mother she'd wanted to be just yet. On the nights she didn't work, she read aloud to Tad for at least half an hour. Sometimes, if it was an extra-exciting part, she might read longer. They were working their way through *Ralph S. Mouse*.

Normally Tad was engrossed in listening, lying stock still with his eyes wide and his lips parted, but tonight he shifted and squirmed, arranging and rearranging his stuffed animals against the pillows beside him. So Perdie wasn't surprised when he laid a hand on her arm to stop her.

"Mommy, why do you have to go to work?"

Perdie sighed. They'd been over this before, and it always left her feeling sick and second-guessing her decision to leave Matt and start over alone. Logically, she knew she'd done the only thing she could to keep her children safe; but emotionally, it wasn't always possible to make that argument. Especially when she hardly even saw her children anymore, and they often acted as if they'd be happier if she weren't around at all.

But she'd try again.

"Well, honey, you know that we have to pay for everything we have with money. When we go to the grocery store, we have to give the store money so they will give us food. I get money by going to work. You don't want us to run out of food, do you?"

Tad looked at her, his brown eyes more serious than she had ever seen them. "Mommy, I don't have to eat. I promise I won't ask for food anymore, if you stay home."

Tad's words and the broken, earnest timbre of his voice sank into Perdie's soul like autumn sunlight sinking to the forest floor: a soft, inevitable illumination that transformed every colour, every leaf, every limb that it touched. She sat there, transfixed in pain for a moment, trying to find words and not tears, so that she could answer her son.

Finally, she managed. "It would make me very sad if you didn't eat, honey. We all need food to live. I don't want you to ever be hungry. And it's my job to take care of you. I wish I could be home more, too. We just have to all pull together and try to take good care of each other when we can."

She could see that her answer was far from satisfactory, but it was the only one she had to give. Still, when she lay on the futon that night, staring at the glow of the streetlights through her thin curtains, his words clung to her, so that all her bones and muscles ached with the weight of them.

Those words cost me a major victory, one I can usually count on when it comes to struggling, single parents. It should have been an immediate, knee-jerk trade of time for security. I was so sure Perdie would chase the acquisition of money and possessions with the same, single-minded devotion of most of you, that I almost wasn't paying as much attention to this moment as I should have been. But she surprised me. She saw possibilities I'd all but forgotten existed.

My default temptations work so well, I hardly ever have to get creative any more. That's on me.

I mean, I so nearly succeeded with the very Son of God. Some people like to point to that story as my greatest failure, but if only you knew how close I came to persuading him, you'd see it differently. You doubt me, don't you?

I'm sure you know the story of the Temptation of Christ. How I took him up and offered him all the power, all the pleasures of the entire world, if he would only deny his god. Most humans I know don't find that story very impressive. They think, "so what? Christ created all that. It all belongs to him, anyway. How could that possibly be a temptation?" For most people, it carries the implication of empty ritual, a contrived play that he and I carried out on a little stage just so he could later claim that he'd been tempted in all ways as a typical human. But you couldn't be more wrong.

You see, from the moment Christ entered Mary's womb, he had exceeded God, exceeded himself, exceeded Heaven, simply by virtue of sharing in the experiences of his own creation. Remember, the realm of the Others is entirely spiritual. Physical sensation, physical pleasure, physical tension, physical anticipation, physical pain, physical fear, physical achievement — it's all a mystery to them. It's not that they are too good for it: it's that they can't do it. Can't comprehend it. Can't feel it.

So for all the suffering — and I'll own, it was fairly terrific — that Christ would endure, he was and remains to this day the only Other who would ever even begin to understand what his creation actually was. What was I offering him? The chance to remain in that place, suspended between heaven and earth, suspended between spirit and flesh, with all the desires of the intellectual mind and all the sensual delights of the flesh. Kind of the place you're in — except, of course, he would have had all power and wealth, too. So, more the kind of place you've always dreamed of.

When Christ refused what I offered, he wasn't refusing a temporary and subordinate level of power in favour of an eternal one. He was refusing cold water sliding over parched lips on a hot, dry day. He was refusing that rush of strength and power that fills your muscles after an intense workout. He was refusing the scent of lilacs and spruce trees on a frosty spring morning. He was refusing the fierce pleasure of a fist striking flesh and feeling it relent. He was refusing the comfort of a friend's embrace when words are not enough. He was refusing the delightful burning disconnect of whiskey hitting the belly. He was refusing the butt of a dog's head against his palm, the stroke of a sarcastic cat against his calf. He was refusing the salt of the sea, the glitter of the desert, the icy loneliness of the summits, the fury of the storm, the constant caress of the wind. He was refusing all the pleasures he had only barely begun to taste, most of which in his thirty years he would never reach.

I was quite impressed by his discipline, myself. Obviously, I'd adopted the opposite course long ago, myself.

I learned something important that day, though. Sometimes the shortcut to vice is through virtue. And this decision of Perdie's made it perfectly clear to me that she fell very neatly into that category. Simple greed would get me nowhere with her. At least, not greed for the treasure I usually trade in. I'd need something more precious.

Most parents, even objectively inferior parents, want to provide for their children. It's one of those hardwired characteristics that can only be overridden with substances or trauma. It's why abusive alcoholics still send $20 on their kids' birthdays. It's why even junkies are sometimes motivated to come home with a bag of store-brand Lucky Charms and ramen and wait for praise for their outstanding parenting impulses. It's why it's so easy for me to convince single parents to work more and more hours for goods that are increasingly intangible, right up to the moment they lose their kids altogether. They never even know, most of the time, that they did it to themselves.

But despite every advantage I clearly had in this situation — bills, housing, medical care, good solid reason — Tad's ridiculous, impossible, pathetic attempt at negotiating for his mother's time won the day. It took a while for me to realise what was happening, and even longer for Perdie to actually pull it off, but she managed.

She managed.

She took the frame I'd so assiduously constructed around her window, raised the glass, and walked right through. She left behind all the choices I'd painstakingly arranged and seized on one I'd hardly perceived. She abandoned the bustling town and its second jobs and its third jobs and moved her kids to a life I didn't anticipate.

I do love to watch you fight. No matter how many times I watch you falter, watch you fall, watch you fail, there is a glory in that moment when you set your mouth, bunch your muscles, and hurl yourself into the fray that is godly beautiful in its innocence.

After all this time, you still imagine that you can win. Sometimes, I almost think you do.

CHAPTER SIX

So, Jakob's Lake it was. Definitely not the move I'd have liked Perdie to make, and honestly, not one I'd even seen coming. Ironically enough, the scene of yet another of my more regrettable losses. Just a few miles away stood the ghost town of Lulu City. Back in the 1800s, a miner named Jakob Rittenhauer had come to Lulu with his wife and six children. In a colossal stroke of bad luck — and possibly some less-than-divine intervention — all seven perished of fever. Jakob himself fell ill as well, but suffering is defined by survivors. Obviously, I needed someone to live.

From an outside perspective, Jakob might look like one of my success stories, but that's because most of you have such a twisted sense of good and evil. Really, I get so tired of those terms. They just don't express reality as it is. You don't have a good understanding of what is real and what isn't. What is permanent and what is temporary. What I offer — what I am always offering — is simply whatever is temporary. I make no claims to the contrary. In fact, if you ask me, I'll tell you it is entirely the temporary nature of pleasure that gives it its seductive appeal.

Don't believe me?

Ask any cheating spouse on the planet — if you can find an honest one. If the first words out of their mouth are something about love or affirmation, keep walking. But an honest one will admit the truth.

Talk to someone who works in a candy factory. Or an ice cream factory. Do they ever eat sweets anymore, or has all the allure vanished?

Do you think people would wax poetic about rainbows if they hung in the sky twenty-four hours a day? If swimming with the dolphins was the only way to get to work in the morning, would you still want to go swimming on the weekends? If snow never melted, would you still go dancing in the snowfall and catch the flakes on your tongue?

Jakob Rittenhauer, in what was the lowest point of his existence, decided to drop out of ordinary life. He left the mine while it was still producing — smart move, actually, as it wasn't exactly a roaring success in the end — and built himself a cabin on the edge of an uninhabited lake. And though I did my best to distract him, to point out the inherent — and temporary — pleasures in alcohol, the sweet escape he could find in death even, he somehow kept his head. Oh, he mourned. He was still close enough to his former home that many afternoons found him seated on the scrub at the Lulu City cemetery, carrying on rambling conversations with the dead.

What he didn't do was despair. And that's why, as more and more people moved across the mountains and met the strange old friendly hermit on the edge of the lake, they couldn't forget him. In fact, he became a landmark. Hence the eventual name of the small town that sprang up there: Jakob's Lake. He surrounded himself with everything most temporary in your world and saw past their ethereal shadows and into their eternal forms. Physically, he barely survived, completely dependent on the ever-changing vagaries of nature for food, for shelter, for all the mundanities you poor creatures require to keep your soul-cages rattling along. But *spiritually, he was out of my reach. He practised birdcalls as if he learned foreign languages, he attended the births of spring fawns in patient concealment, he stayed up late to watch the stars travel their invisible roads. He grieved lost beauties yet still sought and found new ones.*

But no need to dwell on that. Perdie, Tad, Rachel, and Hannah — they were all still well within my grasp. Even if I wasn't exactly thrilled at this latest turn of events. Any time a parent chooses quality of life over quantity of money, I lose ground.

A point to me, though — Hannah and Rachel weren't thrilled, either. This move was even messier than the first one. Perdie's lease was up in March. She still had a little of the nest egg she'd hoarded up before the move, but there was no question of renewing. Not without either getting a second full-time job or winning the lottery. Her monthly paycheque managed to pay the bills, pay the attorney, and a little more, but that little more would never amount to a rent payment in Fort Collins. Very soon she'd be upside-down. In a few weeks, when the divorce was final — if Matt stopped dragging his feet — she'd have a little extra from child support; but a college professor's paycheque wasn't anything outrageous to begin with. She didn't think it would be much, could be much, without bankrupting him. Maybe if her children had been happy, she'd have risked staying and hoping for a financial miracle, but that hadn't been the case.

Perdie didn't know who was worse off, Rachel or Hannah. Coming into a new school two months after the semester had started was bound to be difficult, even if everything else had been wonderful. Rachel, her little people-pleaser, didn't know how to not try too hard. Every day she went to school and turned herself inside-out, and every day she came home heart-broken. She was a pretty little girl. She'd been the only one to inherit Matt's blue eyes, and they simply glowed under her masses of dark hair. She was smart, and sweet, but the other children could smell the unhappiness and desperation on her.

School children aren't like real children — they're like a family pet that has been lost and finds itself running with a pack of now-feral dogs. They exist for the hunt, for that wretched running-down of a wounded beast, for the smell of blood in their nostrils and the taste of flesh in their teeth. Merely a whiff of weakness has them circling their prey.

So, Rachel remained the sad little girl she'd been in that minivan travelling across the country. She made a couple of haphazard friends, but they weren't reliable — at the slightest sign of social risk, they fled, as any child with a scrap of self-preservation will do. So, she began to take refuge in food, while her sister Hannah took refuge in herself.

It wasn't that Hannah didn't want friends. She did. It was that she had figured out long ago the dynamics that Rachel was still fighting, and she had no intention of showing her hand at the table like that. Hannah took all the want, all the loneliness, all the bewilderment, all the try inside herself, and bundled it into a dark, quiet space that she vowed never to look at. She read, and she drew. She kept her head down, and she ghosted through those school halls so successfully that none of her classmates today would recall her face, much less her name. A few might have been intrigued, but she shut them down so effectively with just a hard glance at any approach that no one got any closer than that.

Perdie didn't know any of that, but she did know how quiet and angry her oldest child was becoming. Explosions at home were rare but well worth the ticket price. Perdie knew that her latest decision, to uproot the kids yet again, in the middle of the same school year, would be wildly unpopular; but as far as she could see, things were only getting worse where they were, and she didn't think they could survive, anyway. As hated as she would be, moving her family to Jakob's Lake was her last-ditch effort to save the unsalvageable.

As for Tad? He took on the role of buffer that most often belongs to the middle child. When the girls came home from school, Tad would drag his bag of train tracks into their bedroom and steadily build and build wherever there was a clear spot on the floor. Rachel would nag Hannah for attention, and Hannah would curl up on her bed with her sketchpad and try to pretend she was alone. Eventually, Rachel would give up and go to Jessa. Tad and Hannah would persist in quiet companionship, and occasionally, driven by a solitude too great for any ten-year-old to bear, Hannah would slide down on to the floor and push a train, wishing she could still find the bliss in it that her brother did.

Even unhappy children despise change, and Perdie's new plan was met with fierce resistance. Children are powerless, though, and the move happened regardless of their tears and screaming and fervent arguments. Perdie moved her children from the bustling town of Fort Collins to the tiny hamlet of Jakob's Lake at the end of March.

It was a bigger risk than her children knew. Her department store job, even with its low pay, had at least offered health insurance, which was a constant concern with three young children. While Fort Collins was glutted with over-qualified job applicants, she'd known that if worst came to worst, she could always get a job at a McDonald's or a KFC or a Starbucks. Jakob's Lake boasted no such promise. A few restaurants and bars, a few tourist shops, a few recreational businesses, and the ever-present real estate offices didn't leave a lot of positions open for newcomers. There was no hospital and no museums, unless you counted the little preserved cabin next to the visitor centre that boasted itself the home of the town's namesake.

But the advantages were new and marvellous. Set on the verge of a crystal blue lake shadowed by mountain peaks and towering firs, the little town of Jakob's Lake petered out into wilderness on every side. Although the children would have to be bussed away to a central high school when the time came, a small combined elementary and middle school was within walking distance of the little apartment Perdie had secured at a much lower price than what she'd had to pay in Fort Collins. Of course, the apartment was smaller, too — only a two bedroom instead of three, with no balcony.

As for work, Perdie had convinced a local that he not only needed her, but he needed her well before the tourist season started. Justin Nilsson owned Viking Kayaks, the sole kayak enterprise on the lake. The job only ran through October, but Perdie had dismissed all the rational arguments and taken the chance anyway. God only knows what her plan was.

Jakob's Lake didn't run on the sort of schedule and expectations of the city, and Justin wasn't fazed by the prospect of Perdie's kids hanging around the shop, as long as they didn't get in the way and didn't drown. That was a huge plus for Perdie. Lack of health insurance was a huge minus. But she had a plan. She was hoping to negotiate for Matt's university-provided health insurance to continue to cover the kids. Even if that meant she got less support every month, it would be worth it. And if that didn't pan out, she would swallow her pride and go to the state for help. The only good thing about her newly reduced paycheque was that she was officially poor, which gave her a few options. However little she might want them.

The rest is details. All those incredibly petty, mundane minutiae on which you hang the whole of your expectations, while the gusto and grief of life pass you by unnoticed. Just thinking about them now bores me silly. God is the one who pays attention to that nonsense. Every sparrow that falls and all the hairs of your head and all that. I'm here for the rollercoaster, baby, for the lights and the colours and the screams.

So, we're going to fast-forward a bit. I could tell you everything you've missed, but I think you'll catch on pretty quickly to most of it. Perdie and Justin ended up as best friends, and Justin and his husband, Alan, spent many winter evenings with her and the kids, even after she got a full-time job at the Chamber of Commerce. She married Reilly Rodriguez, another work-in-progress for me, as I like to refer to my present failures, and everyone got older. Even Matt Blevins went on with his life, and in a fashion I fully endorsed.

So let's turn the page, shall we? Everyone knows the fairy tale doesn't get interesting until after the happy ending.

CHAPTER SEVEN

"Hey, honey." Even through the phone, Reilly sounded distracted to her.

"Hey, honey." Perdie drawled her response as sarcastically as possible. "Guess who I just got off the phone with?"

"Umm ... who?"

"Hannah. Can you guess what she had to tell me?"

"Oh." She could tell she had his full attention now. She pictured her slight, wiry husband straightening up, pushing his glasses back, as he shifted gears from whatever electronics project he had laid out on the counter of his small shop, Rodriguez Electronics and Appliance Repair, to what he now realised was his irate wife on the phone.

"Yeah, 'oh'," she mimicked his sad attempt at stalling. "How long have you known that she'd dropped out of school?"

Reilly sighed. "Maybe we should wait till I get home to talk about this."

"Justin and Alan are coming over for dinner, remember?"

"They're practically family, anyway."

"Are you going to tell me that they knew, too?"

"No, no, no. At least, I don't think so. I just meant, we don't exactly keep a lot of secrets from them, anyway."

"Maybe not, but I still don't want to subject them to our disagreements. How long have you known?"

"Perdie ... ah, you're going be so mad. Listen, I told her she needed to tell you right away. It just took her a while to work up the nerve."

"To work up the nerve? To talk to her own mother? You guys make me sound like a monster."

"It's not that, honey. You know Hannah loves you. It's just ... she doesn't want to disappoint you. She knows how much it meant to you that she go to college, especially since you didn't."

"But she wasn't worried about disappointing you."

"It's different, babe. You know that. I've only been her dad for eight years. You've been her mom for her whole life. She has a lot of respect for you."

"Is that what you call it? Lying to me, deceiving me? Jeopardising her entire future? And what about you? How could you not tell me?"

"I promised her I'd let her be the one to break the news to you. Of course, I thought she was going to do that much sooner than she did, and, in retrospect, I can see that was a poor promise to make, but—"

"How. Long. Reilly."

A moment of hesitation. Then, quietly: "We talked it over before she dropped out. At the end of September."

Perdie sputtered, momentarily short-circuited by rage.

Reilly rushed to fill the void. "I'm so sorry. I should have told you right away. I was trying to do right by both of you, and I get that I missed the mark on that. But I swear, this wasn't a malicious impulse on either of our parts. We weren't trying to hurt you or disrespect you."

"Well. As long as you weren't being malicious, then. I guess that makes it all better. I'm sure you need to get back to work. We can discuss this more later."

"Okay, I—"

Perdie disconnected the call.

She pushed a shaking hand through her long, silver-shot brown hair. At this rate, it was going to be all silver by the end of the week, she thought. She hated arguing with Reilly. She didn't have enough practice to be good at it, she told herself in a failed attempt at humour. Reilly was steady, kind, calm, unselfish — all the qualities that her first husband had lacked. He was patient, too, a virtue that had come in handy in the first few years of their marriage. Perdie had picked up more than a handful of unhealthy habits born out of her experiences as a battered wife, and she'd unconsciously attempted to sabotage her new marriage more than once or twice.

It had taken quite a while before she realised that she and Reilly could argue, that they could even outright fight, and still no one would get hurt, no one would need to feel afraid, and no one would leave. Reilly was probably regretting how sincerely he'd convinced her of that about now, she considered drily.

It was impossible for her to stay mad at him, and she knew it. Honestly, that was at least half of why she'd called him right away, because otherwise, she'd have calmed down by the time he got home, and he'd have never borne the brunt of her wrath — which was important. She didn't want him thinking it was a good idea to go ahead keeping secrets with the kids behind her back. But deep down, she knew that his heart had been absolutely true, that he'd been trying to be the best dad he could be, which was one of the reasons she loved him as the best husband that he was.

Not that they argued much. To be honest, she didn't know

anyone — with the possible exception of Justin and Alan — who were just disgustingly happy, who was still as in love with their spouse after eight years of marriage as she and Reilly were. And she privately thought that Justin and Alan had cheated the system, really, by not having kids, who had to be the source of at least sixty percent of all married couples' disagreements. Justin and Alan weren't just childless — they were blissfully childless, with no intention of changing that state. Alan had said more than once that he considered the impossibility of an unplanned pregnancy one of the huge advantages of their relationship, and Perdie could never tell if he was joking or not.

Right now, she was tempted to envy them. What was Hannah thinking? Dropping out of college halfway through a teaching degree to become an apprentice in a tattoo shop? It was like something out of a reality TV show. A book of parenting horror stories that moms giggled over in dentists' waiting rooms and never imagined could happen to them in real life.

And Reilly had known all along. Perdie dropped her head in her hands. That made her sick to her stomach. She had felt betrayed the moment Reilly had confessed, but that wasn't it. It was just ... ugh. If only she'd known when he'd known, maybe she could have stopped Hannah before she dropped out. Before she lost an entire semester of study, to what? What did a tattoo apprentice do, anyway? Clean needles and pass out colouring books? There was no way Hannah could make enough money to live on that, was there? Perdie had no idea how much money a tattoo artist made, she realised.

In fact, she'd never even been in a tattoo shop. The closest experience she'd had was watching the occasional reality show when nothing else was on TV. Reilly had a tattoo on his shoulder from when he was about twenty or so, but she'd never thought much about it. Perdie didn't think tattoo shops looked like places with wildly successful people working inside. And what kind of customers did they have? She imagined a parade of ex-cons, motorcycle outlaws, white supremacists, and dancing girls.

Even in the midst of her panic-fuelled ire, she laughed. Okay, clearly there was a hysterical edge to her thinking. She was sure plenty of nice people got tattoos, too. Actually, Julie Chambers had just posted a photo last week of a string of flowers she'd had tattooed on her foot. Perdie had thought she was crazy — why on earth would anyone pay somebody to colour on them with a needle? But it had been pretty enough, and she'd made appreciative noises about it.

But Hannah — Hannah was so smart, so talented. She'd always had something burning in her that her mother didn't quite understand but stood in awe of, a fire that set her apart. She was so quiet, so perfectly contained, her beauty understated but flawless, so that everyone felt the energy shift when she entered a room and when she left it. It was a flame that people admired from a distance rather than attempted to warm themselves at, and Perdie often worried that her daughter was too lonely, too isolated. Who knew she'd been busy making friends with tattoo artists?

Oh, crumbs. Weren't those piercing people usually in tattoo shops, too? Was Hannah going to come home not only covered in ink but riddled with holes?

"How is this happening?" she groaned aloud.

"You okay, Perdie?"

Perdie's head snapped around. She'd been so absorbed in her thoughts, she hadn't even heard the jingle of bells over the door where she was working. Hazel Jenkins was looking at her anxiously, her white hair wildly askew from walking the mail door to door in the cold November wind. Bright pink earmuffs were a stark contrast to her staid blue postal-office uniform.

"Oh, I'm sorry, Hazel. Just ... kids, you know?"

Hazel nodded vigorously, her worried expression breaking into a relieved smile. "Oh, yes, I definitely do know. You don't think I got this white hair from being old, do you?"

Perdie laughed. "I can't think of a safe response to that question."

"Fair, fair." Hazel stomped her feet, taking advantage of the few moments indoors to warm up her legs. "Try not to fret too much. They all gotta go their own way, no matter what we think. And your kids are good people. They won't go too far off the rails."

Hazel probably had ten tattoos, Perdie thought wryly. No doubt she'd be thrilled to hear that Hannah was going to be an ink artist. Aloud she said, "Yeah, I know you're right. It's not like they've killed anyone. Even if I do feel like they're about to send me to an early grave sometimes."

"Exactly." Hazel nodded again. "It's all relative, hon. You hang in there! I'll see you later."

A jingle of bells and a gust of cold air, and Perdie was alone again. She stood up, rubbing her hands briskly together, and crossed the room to look out the big plate windows that faced the town's namesake. Peace gusted through her at the sight of the rugged mountains rising over the lake, its not-quite-frozen blue waters sluggish in the early-morning cold.

I'll admit, my interest in Perdie was purely academic at this point. Just a handful of choices, rather than any daily vigilance on her part, kept her mostly out of my reach. She was so well-knotted in the warp and weft of her relationships. Untangling those strings, getting her alone, was going to require quite a change of circumstance. Once having decided to pursue time with her children and a more peaceful life over money and security, she didn't spend time regretting what she'd lost out on. It had taken some effort on Reilly's part to convince her that he was the right man to bring into her home and into her children's hearts, but once he had, she'd never been tempted by anyone else. So, even as agitated as she was feeling now, Perdie wasn't a target for me.

Not yet.

CHAPTER EIGHT

Dinner was comfortably hectic, the usual Monday night affair. During the off-season months, when the lake was too cold or too frozen for kayaking, Justin and Alan came over for a standing taco night every Monday. Or at least, Justin did. Alan was a deputy sheriff for the county, and Perdie had never been able to make sense of his schedule. So sometimes he showed, and sometimes he didn't. Tonight, he did.

At fourteen and seventeen, Tad and Rachel were mostly too cool to hang out with their parents, but even they made an exception on Monday nights. Reilly hadn't been exaggerating when he'd said that the Nilssons were practically family. Tad and Rachel had called them Uncle Justin and Uncle Alan almost since they'd moved to Jakob's Lake. The two men had had immediate appeal for the children when they'd first met — after all, one of them was a super-buff master of kayaking and all things outdoor, and the other one was a cop. The fact that they'd instantly adopted Perdie and her three broken-hearted children as their own had only cemented their cool factor.

Hannah and Rachel had made little effort to conceal their hopeless crushes on Justin, who'd been kind enough to hide his amusement from them if not from their mother. Tad and the slightly less fit Alan had hit it off on a more intellectual level, bonding over their shared interests in video games and science fiction. Alan was open about his dyslexia, a struggle which fascinated the avid reader Tad. Many a night between the two had been spent in passionate movie-versus-book arguments. It wasn't unusual for Alan to stop by the house while on patrol, ostensibly for a cup of coffee or to steal a cookie or two, a habit that had begun back when Perdie first moved to town and needed all the help she could get.

Taco night had actually been Reilly's idea, back when he'd first started dating Perdie, and had rapidly expanded to include the Nilssons. The whole point had been to give Perdie a night off from cooking dinner for the kids, and that part of the tradition still held, too. Tad was the house vegetable chopper, an undertaking that had been considerably more perilous when he was only six. There'd been more than one bloody mishap, but Reilly had insisted it was good for Tad to learn, and Perdie had to admit there'd been no loss of limb. Hannah had been responsible for cooking the meat, and Rachel, the family's entertaining expert, had the task of setting out and organising all the plates, glasses, condiments, and taco shells.

Cleaning up had fallen to Reilly, who'd since taken up the cooking portion, as well, once Hannah moved back to Fort Collins to attend Colorado State University. After he and Perdie had gotten married, Reilly cooked more often than one night a week, but taco night remained sacrosanct.

Rattled by the day's news, Perdie was grateful for the familiar flow of the weekly ritual. When she came in the door at 5:30, the sound of animated voices and clattering flatware comforted her. Reilly rounded the corner to greet her, wiping his hands on a hand towel. His brown eyes regarded her anxiously from behind wire-rimmed glasses.

"Hi, honey. How was the rest of your day?"

It was hardly fair, Perdie considered, that she couldn't stay mad at him. She ought to at least make him squirm a little longer, but she couldn't resist putting him out of his misery.

"Other than our rapscallion daughter, it was fine," she told him, kissing his cheek. She felt the tension ease out of him at her touch. "One of these days, though, I'm going to learn how to carry a grudge, and then you'll be in trouble."

Her husband was careful to maintain an appropriately abashed expression, but she knew him too well to imagine his fear ran more than skin-deep. "I know, I know. I did bring home a pizza-sized chocolate chip cookie from the grocery store, if that helps."

"Reilly!" She laughed, any lingering austerity vanishing at the promise of her favourite treat. "You know Justin and Alan are bringing dessert."

"I know, but this was urgent. I wanted to make sure there was no danger of running out of enough chocolate. What if they bring vanilla ice cream or something?"

Perdie nodded. "Excellent point. You did well."

Reilly grinned, the ready creases transforming his face from sombre to infectious joy. Perdie felt her own spirits rise to meet his, wondering for the thousandth time what on earth his ex-wife, Melia, had been thinking, divorcing a man like this one solely for the sake of bearing her own biological children. What a fool, to throw away a sure and faithful love on the chance of an ephemeral hope.

Perdie at least had the grace of hating her ex-husband. Reilly hadn't had it so easy.

Like Perdie, he'd married his high school sweetheart. They'd waited, though, till they both graduated from college, both with engineering degrees. Melia's had been oil and gas, Reilly's, of course, was electrical. They'd both gotten good jobs in Denver, lived in a beautiful apartment with a balcony garden, and life, blissfully hectic, seemed idyllic.

That's one of my best lines, as it turns out: "without all those terrible mistakes..." It's pathetically easy to convince you that any number of terrible decisions were necessary to bring you to some random present happiness. Most of you don't have the vaguest concept of quantum theory, but you've all embraced butterfly theory when it comes to justifying your own terrible mistakes. I mean, there are a hundred ways to arrive at Jakob's Lake, for instance. Nothing necessitates you taking the route with the most possible heartbreak along the way.

But hey. Broken-road platitudes make for great country songs and help keep me in business, so ...

My chance to intervene in Reilly's relationship hadn't come for five years, when they'd decided they wanted children. Neither of them knew what I did: Reilly was sterile. And it's a feature of the engineering personality that they can sometimes be exceptionally particular. Melia was quite particular about what she wanted: a natural pregnancy, with her husband's baby.

Weird, right? I mean, especially now, when you have worked out a half-dozen solutions to the problems of childlessness (if you really want to call that a problem). Reilly, never having experienced the expectation of having a child growing inside him, had not been nearly so particular. He'd tried and tried to convince Melia to adopt. He'd even been willing to attempt artificial insemination, with a stranger supplying the sperm.

But Melia had been adamant about what she wanted. So, she'd left. Left him, still loving him. And he'd had no choice but to watch the woman he still loved walk away. All for the sake of a fairy tale Melia had told herself in her head since she was a child.

That's a whole different sort of loose ends situation than most people have to live with. It's one thing when a relationship ends in hatred or contempt or even pity. But when the relationship ends, and the love goes on ... please, people. Even I have a hard time watching that. It leaves this permanent, unfinished feeling in my stomach. I'm always looking over my shoulder, waiting for the subplot to re-emerge.

Reilly probably felt the same way, because he bailed on the life he'd had with Melia in every possible way. He'd left Denver and headed for the tiny hamlet of Jakob's Lake with a big wad of cash and no real plans at all. They'd been saving for a house since they moved to Denver, after all, and with the divorce they just split everything down the middle. He'd opened an electrical repair shop and bought a family-size cabin on the edge of town fairly cheaply, because with winter coming on, real estate prices were dropping. Likely, he was still hoping at that point that Melia would change her mind and come back, maybe even with an adopted child or two in tow.

But Melia hadn't. I might not have made many successful inroads with Reilly, but his first wife was a different matter. That being so particular is always going to be a point in my favour. It's not a survival characteristic, you know, being particular. One of humanity's greatest evolutionary features is your adaptability, your nimbleness, your flexibility. Ironically, the more control you gain over your environment, the more protections you create, the more brittle and intractable you become.

I think most of you would freeze to death wandering around in a blizzard hunting for a cell phone signal so you could call search and rescue before you found shelter, even though your kind has been surviving and thriving in the harshest of winters for thousands of years. Certainly you'd rather die of the plague and take everyone you can with you before going without your requisite morning latte or those sun-dried tomatoes at your favourite market.

But I digress. This isn't Melia's story. It's not even Reilly's. Let's go on.

The slam of a car door and a murmur of low voices outside meant Justin and Alan had arrived. Perdie followed Reilly into the kitchen, knowing that the two men would let themselves in and wander into the kitchen at their leisure. Besides, she needed a minute to change into jeans and a T-shirt before they started slinging tacos. She'd learned the hard way that tacos and dress clothes never mixed.

Chips, salsa, guac, cheese, taco shells, ground beef, and all the fixings were arranged buffet-style, and everyone piled their plates high and retired to the living room to gorge themselves and dispense the latest news. The kids always plied Alan for his latest arrests, though the county in which Jakob's Lake was located was hardly a crime metropolis. Something entertaining always seemed to happen, nonetheless.

Tonight, though, Perdie was anxious to discuss the topic that had been plaguing her all day, hoping against hope that Justin or Alan would have some brilliant idea that would convince Hannah to go back to school before she covered every inch of her skin with ink and hung a chain from her chin to her cheek.

"So, I have some news," she broke in, as soon as Alan finished his story about getting called out to rescue a real estate agent from an angry bull. All eyes turned toward her.

"Hannah called me today. She's dropped out of school. Moved into an apartment with a couple of strangers. Three strangers, actually. She probably sleeps in a kitchen cupboard. And she is working as an apprentice at a tattoo shop."

She almost — but not quite — missed the furtive glance skating between Rachel and Tad.

"Hey!" she exclaimed, her ire returning. "Did you already know?"

Rachel shrugged guiltily, not meeting her mother's eyes.

Tad swallowed his bite of taco convulsively, meeting his mother's accusing gaze with a wry smile and a slight shrug. "We didn't know, exactly. At least, I didn't. Not for sure," he told her. "We're just not surprised."

"How could your sister becoming a tattoo artist not surprise you?" Perdie could hear her voice rising to a yelp, but modulating it was beyond her at the moment.

Rachel choked on a snicker but kept her face down. Alan and Justin watched raptly. Reilly quietly got up and went to the kitchen to refill his plate. Tad was the only one who seemed unaffected by his mother's impending hysteria.

"You had to know she hated school," Tad told Perdie matter-of-factly. "She'd have been a terrible teacher. She gets tired after a ten-minute conversation. There's no way she'd make it through a day of teaching classes. And she's a fantastic artist."

"I didn't know she hated school!" Perdie insisted, but her voice sounded unconvincing even to her own ears. Had she known? Probably. But she had wanted — needed — Hannah to push through it. To get that diploma. To have a real chance at making it in life. To have options Perdie hadn't had.

"She only had two years left," she said weakly.

"Two more years doing what she hated," Tad told her flatly. "Two years can be a lifetime."

"But ... a tattoo artist? Do they even make any money? It's not like there's some advancement possibilities with a job like that. Or insurance. Or benefits. And she doesn't even have any tattoos!"

A hastily muffled sound from the couch had her swinging to face Justin and Alan. Poker-faced Alan had just punched

Justin, who was fighting an unsuccessful battle to bring his features under control.

"What?" barked Perdie exasperatedly. "She has a tattoo? And you two know about it, and I don't?"

Justin gave up, his handsome face breaking into a wide grin. "Oh, does she, though. It's a pin-up gorilla on the side of her upper thigh."

Perdie buried her face in her hands. "Oh, dear Lord."

"She said it was ironic," Justin went on gleefully.

"I'm beginning to find motherhood ironic," she muttered.

Reilly's hand fell on her shoulder. "Here," he said gently. "Have some cookie."

She laughed reluctantly. "You know cookies don't fix everything. They definitely don't fix gorilla tattoos."

"Sure they do," Alan told her. "By the time you finish your cookie, you'll realise that she hasn't started shooting heroin or killed anyone. She's just taken a different path than expected. And she may not even stay on this path. She's only twenty. She can change her mind as often as she wants. She'll be okay, Perdie."

Reilly had taken the time to heat up the cookie in the microwave. Warm chocolate and sugar burst on Perdie's tongue, mouth-watering and oddly reassuring. Still, she had too much self-respect to give in that easily. "Sure, sure," she grumbled. "And Rachel's going to run off to join the circus, and Tad's going to live in our basement playing video games forever. But it's all good, Perdie."

"Hey!" Tad piped up defensively. Clearly his laissez-faire attitude did not extend to his own prospects. "First of all, we don't even have a basement. Secondly, I'm going to be a NASA engineer. I've got plans."

"What about me?" Rachel demanded indignantly, glaring at her little brother.

He bit into his taco and lifted a shoulder. "I figured you'd love to join the circus, based on that clown makeup you like to wear."

"Okay, okay!" Perdie propelled herself into motion, pulling Rachel away from her little brother before his tacos ended up all over the carpet. "I get it. I'm overreacting, and everyone else is cool with our oldest and her pin-up gorilla. Rachel, you do not look like a clown. Your brother is just being obnoxious because he can."

She gave Tad a firm look, but he grinned irrepressibly at her around yet another mouthful. Rachel contented herself with fulminating glares and a grade-A hair flip that would have made any runway model proud.

Justin saved the night with an abrupt change of subject.

"So — we're going to Mexico."

"What? When?"

"For Christmas, actually. Much as we love Mom and Dad, we couldn't face another East Coast trip this year. A little sand and surf was an easy sell."

Justin's parents lived in Maine, and whenever they could, Justin and Alan flew back there for a visit. Alan came from a long family of deeply conservative law enforcement, and to say that they hadn't made their peace with his marriage would be an understatement. They'd endure an occasional stiff family dinner, but a holiday would be insufferable. As Alan said, he'd never put Justin through that. Justin's family, though taken aback, had welcomed Alan with open arms, and the only distance between them was geographical.

"And you're actually getting Christmas off?" Reilly asked Alan. "That's practically a Christmas miracle right there."

Alan laughed. "Well, no, of course not. I have to work through the 26th. But we leave town on the 27th, and we don't come home till January 8th. So we're calling it Christmas in Mexico."

Perdie wasn't surprised. She thought Alan might have had actual Christmas Day off twice in the years since she'd moved here, and one of those years he'd had to go in anyway when a terrible car accident had meant all hands on deck. Luckily Justin was easy-going and always seemed unruffled by the inconsistencies of his partner's schedule.

"That sounds amazing!" Rachel had dropped her air of dudgeon. "I wish we could go to Mexico. Reilly, you should take us to Mexico. For heritage."

Reilly nearly choked on a tortilla chip. "Heritage? Rachel, you know my dad's family has been in the US for ages. My great-grandpa was the immigrant. I don't even speak Spanish."

"But don't you want to know about your family history? We should go."

Perdie grinned, enjoying her husband being stuck in the hot seat instead of her for a change. "Yeah, honey. We should all go to the Old Country. Find some long-lost cousins."

Reilly shot her a look that promised later retribution. "I'm pretty sure my family wasn't from Cabo or Cancun, pumpkin," he said, using the nickname he'd had for Rachel since she was little. "If we went looking for my roots, we'd wind up in farming country somewhere, and farm country is equally exciting the world over."

Rachel rolled her eyes. "Well, we wouldn't have to stay there," she persisted. "We could meet an old grandma or something and then go to the beach, surf, and drink margaritas."

Reilly laughed outright at that. "You've never surfed in your life. And you're seventeen. No margaritas for you."

"I can learn! And fine. But I can have an umbrella in my lemonade."

"How about Galveston?" Tad put in. "That's a beach. That's south. And it's right by Houston and NASA's space centre."

"You two do realise we aren't actually planning a family trip tonight, don't you?" Perdie inserted hastily before they got too carried away.

"I'm just saying," Tad said. "Give you something to think about. Maybe if we all went on a trip together, you could get some time with Hannah to talk about her future."

Perdie lobbed a broken piece of her taco shell at Tad. He ducked, and it sailed into her husband's lap instead. Reilly picked it up smoothly and tossed it into his mouth.

"That was pathetic," Perdie told her son. He grinned at her.

"I have to play the hand I'm given. I'm just trying to get you to see all the advantages here. And if you take me to the space centre, I'll probably be so inspired that I'll get straight As all through high school and earn a full scholarship. Then you'll have one kid you can be proud of."

"Hey, what about me?" Rachel squeaked.

"We love you, Rachel, but circus clowns just don't make the family Christmas letter."

Perdie was too slow to block Rachel's wrath this time. Tad flew backwards with a whoomph, shredded lettuce and cheese flying everywhere.

CHAPTER NINE

Later that night, Perdie murmured into the darkness, her arm flung across her husband's bare chest.

"I hate to admit it, but maybe Tad was on to something. Maybe we should think about one more family trip. It would probably be the last time we all travel together. The kids are growing up so fast."

I'm always fascinated by your compulsion toward movement. By my reckoning, Perdie had only been settled in Jakob's Lake for a minute or two, and already she hungered for some new horizon, some stranger vista. You're such an unsettled lot. Tethered to this clay ball, you bounce along its surface, restive and dissatisfied, searching for a wilderness that all along lies within. But I'd be the last one to tell you that. And it's an odd irony, isn't it? God spent so much time pouring Their own nature and energy and beauty into a creation they were going to caution you not to love too much from the beginning, and of course you are driven endlessly to its exploration. Seems tricky to me.

"Maybe." Reilly sounded unconvinced and more than halfway asleep. "But when? Tad and Rachel are in school. I doubt we'd be able to persuade Hannah to take time off from her apprenticeship right after starting. And the holidays are an awful time to travel. And what would we do with Dandelion? I don't think he'd enjoy the trip."

Dandelion, their boxer rescue, was currently snoring on the memory-foam bed Reilly had bought him for Christmas last year in deference of his creeping arthritis. As soon as the chance had come along to adopt a dog, she'd leapt at it. Matt would never have allowed an animal in the house. So when Hannah had come home with the boxer puppy she'd found in an alley just a few weeks after the move to Jakob's Lake, Perdie hadn't put up a fight at all.

Hannah had been the one to hopefully christen the gangly puppy Ajax, but that had lasted no time at all. He was scared of cars, scared of thunderstorms, scared of knocks on the door. His one skill seemed to be tearing up weeds in the yard, so Tad had insisted on calling him Dandelion, much to his sister's dismay. Now he was nine years old, slightly more mature, slightly less scared. Slightly.

Perdie bit her lip and burrowed more deeply into Reilly's warmth, breathing in the earthy smell of him like an aromatherapy candle.

"That's true. But I don't want to wait too late. If Hannah doesn't register for classes soon, she's going to miss an entire year of college."

Reilly stroked her hair clumsily, more of a pat than a caress. "Honey, I think you're going to have to make your peace with a year off school. Maybe Hannah will change her mind and go back later, but she seems pretty determined on this course."

"So what do we do? Just let her throw her future away?"

"Ummm ... yeah. Maybe. Trade it in, at least, for a future she really wants. Odds are good this won't work out for her. But think about how many things in our early lives didn't work out for us. We found a way through. And probably no one could have changed our minds at the time. Without all those terrible mistakes, we'd have never made it here."

Perdie and Reilly had fallen silent, no doubt both thinking about the routes they had taken to each other.

CHAPTER TEN

Perdie thought her heart might burst as she pulled into the drive. Surrounded by a natural fence of dark green firs with their black trunks, Tad and Reilly were bare-armed in the frosty air, raking up heaps of jewel-coloured leaves and shoving them into giant paper sacks. She could see Tad's lips moving and had no doubt he'd been filling Reilly's ears since he'd gotten home from school. Reilly's face was relaxed, his usual easy-going smile playing on his lips as he tossed more leaves toward Tad.

Perdie didn't know how she'd gotten so lucky, and she had no intention of tempting fate by asking.

Tempting fate is such a delightful turn of phrase. The Fates are just somebody the Greeks made up to explain their own miseries, whereas I'm quite real. Not that the Greeks came up with the notion first — theirs was just the name that stuck. But I'll answer to it, most happily. Go ahead. Tempt me. I love a good game of chicken.

Reilly couldn't possibly be more different than Matt.

Although both men were highly intelligent, Matt would have considered menial work beneath him. Reilly wasn't just willing to tackle any sort of physical labour, he enjoyed it, thrived on it. He'd often said how much happier he was out here rather than in the city going from office to car to apartment to car to office. Perdie knew that his talents were somewhat wasted on Jakob's Lake, but he'd made himself an integral part of the little community since long before she'd arrived.

Much more important than their intellectual differences, though, was the difference in temperament between Matt and Reilly. Reilly saved his tendencies toward perfection for his shop. There, every component, every tool, had its own little drawer, neatly labelled. He cleaned his workstation several times a day and had a precise, regimented approach to every job he tackled, no matter how big or small. At home, though, he had more patience than Perdie for the endless chaos summoned by three children.

And strangest of all, she never had to worry about a flying hand or an ugly, screaming mouth thrust in her face. It had taken a long, long time for Perdie's stomach to stop clenching up every time they disagreed, to overcome the inclination to put a table or a couch between them when Reilly's mood was blue or black. He'd been patient, persistent, unafraid of all her fears and her broken systems, certain that in time he could help her heal them all. And he very nearly had.

Not only that, but Reilly had no difficulty whatsoever loving another man's children as his own. And her three had been exceptionally pitiful when he'd met them. Hannah, completely withdrawn and distrustful; Rachel, broken-hearted and confused; and Tad, unhesitatingly affectionate and hungry for male approval. Even as much as Perdie had protected them from the full truth of her marriage, they'd all been a little shell-shocked, a little anxious, and ready for disaster to strike at any moment.

(It's a funny paradox: the fear and apprehension that leave you most susceptible to my suggestions are the same qualities most thoroughly tamed by love.)

So just as he had with their mother, Reilly quietly and steadily put in the time and wore down their defences.

He had the time because, once Matt realised that his family was largely out of his reach, he'd lost interest. There had been a few scary months in the beginning, when bluster and threats had saturated all his communication, and Perdie had doubted whether she'd ever be free. But Matt had eventually found a woman closer to home whom he could control with far less effort, and his interactions with his children became limited to rare phone calls and even rarer visits. These days, he hardly even remembered their birthdays. Although the children still called Reilly by his name, he had become their dad in every way that mattered.

So today, when Perdie saw her son and her husband raking leaves together on a late-autumn day in the shadow of the mountains, happiness flooded her eyes, and she couldn't help feeling that her whole life was simply too good to be true.

She was right, of course. But no need to dwell on that now.

"Hey, guys," she called as she closed the car door behind her. "Looks like you might actually get that done before the snow falls! Where's Rachel?"

Reilly's face darkened slightly, and Tad was the one to answer. "Probably still upstairs in her room."

"How come? Girls can rake leaves, too."

Tad's lips twisted, his eyes sparking with anger. "Bad bus ride again. You know, I can beat up the guys for her, but the girls ..." His words trailed off.

Perdie exerted fierce control over her own expression. She was torn between amusement at her son's assertion and anger on her daughter's behalf. Tad was all gangly limbs and raw knuckles. She doubted he could beat up a wild turkey, but she appreciated his willingness to try for his sister's sake.

"The girls can be twice as mean as the boys," she finished for him. "I know. I'll go talk to her."

Stepping into her husband's embrace for a quick kiss on the cheek, she was startled into a short laugh when he reached around and squeezed her butt. "I guess you two will have to finish up here on your own. I'll call you when dinner's done."

Perdie dropped her purse and jacket on the dining room table as she came in. When she'd first moved to Colorado, little things like that had been deliberate acts of rebellion, hard-won liberties regained from years of abuse. Now she didn't think twice, and if Reilly came in and made exasperated noises at her mess, she only laughed and cleaned up without a quiver of the terror that had once ruled her limbs.

Now she sighed and brushed back her hair as she headed upstairs. She suspected she knew what the problem was — what it always seemed to be these days. Bubbly, extroverted, empathetic Rachel had been unstoppable in elementary school, till Perdie wished she wouldn't try quite so hard. With the middle and elementary schools combined in Jakob's Lake, Rachel had actually made the dreaded puberty transition with relative ease as the kids who'd resisted her early overtures were either won over or worn down, Perdie wasn't sure which. But once Rachel had started being bussed over to the county high school, all that had changed. The extra pounds that hadn't seemed to matter before now defined her as the "fat girl".

And Rachel tried so hard to be pretty, her mother reflected fretfully. She was the only one of the three children who had Perdie's dark hair and Matt's blue eyes, a striking combination that she played to perfection with professional-level hair and makeup skills. Glossy, shoulder-length curls set off the outfits she chose with such care. Rachel's dream was to be a fashion designer, stylist to the stars, and she regularly scoured the town's one thrift shop hunting for treasures she could restyle, reimagine, redesign into something at once flattering and unique. Rachel wasn't just some wannabe-Kardashian: she was an artist, with an eye and a gift for colour and design.

Unfortunately, in high school, that meant she couldn't convince anyone that she wasn't trying. And nothing signalled blood in the water to the sharks that were high school girls like someone trying.

Rachel did have an extra twenty pounds on her, no doubt. She'd been a tiny thing when they moved to Colorado, but where Hannah had turned to her art for comfort and Tad had turned to his mother, Rachel found solace in her stomach. And she'd been so sad, so lonely, so bewildered, that Perdie hadn't had the heart to deny her little girl anything that would make her feel better.

Perdie knocked softly on her daughter's closed door.

"Come in," came the reluctant response.

Rachel sat hunched under the covers on her bed. She'd already changed out of her clothes and into the fluffy pyjamas that made her look about five years old to her mother. Her cheeks were red and puffy, streaked with mascara. In her right hand, she clutched her cell phone.

"Oh, honey." Perdie sank on to the bed and attempted to

draw her daughter into her arms, wanting to hold her till all the pain went away. "I'm so sorry. Those kids are idiots."

But Rachel resisted, pulling away and wrapping her arms defensively around herself. "Don't, Mom," she protested in a thick voice. "It doesn't help. And they're not idiots, anyway. They're right. I am fat."

"Rachel ..." Perdie began helplessly. She hardly knew where to begin. "First of all, you're not fat. Almost everyone's weight goes up and down, all their life. Second, even if you were a hundred pounds overweight, that wouldn't justify the way those girls are treating you. Your worth and value as a human being isn't based on what you look like or how well you fit into a pair of jeans."

"Oh, super helpful, Mom. I'll be sure to tell them that." Rachel rolled her eyes and then struck a falsetto. "My mommy says I have intrinsic worth as a person, so there."

Perdie sighed. She supposed she deserved that, but she had no idea what she could say or do that would help. She wished she could get that phone away from her daughter. She had a strong suspicion the bullying didn't end when Rachel got off the bus. But it didn't feel fair to cut Rachel off from communication with the few friends she did have, either. At least, Perdie hoped Rachel still had a few friends left, that they hadn't all abandoned her when her social status became a liability.

Desperately, she wondered what the right answer was. Like everyone else, she read the seemingly weekly stories about a child dying by suicide because of bullying. And cyberbullying, in particular, seemed out of control. With the internet, children had no escape, no refuge. Even at home, the ugliness, the meanness, the taunts chased them and cornered them, leaving them with no way out. But what could she do that wouldn't isolate Rachel further?

As an aside, I must admit I'm as ambivalent about social media as the Pope is. I mean, sure, the internet allows me to set up innumerable crossroads for you that would otherwise be impossible. But oh, my darlings, everything I love so much about this beautiful, delicious, madcap, momentary world breathes only in its experience, not its pretence. It saddens me to watch you scrolling Pinterest for cupcake recipes when my hands are full of blackberries, ripe for tasting. In the instant you line up your selfie shot all the archangels are seen burning in the last rays of the sunset. You hunt eBay for plastic figurines while I invite you to dip your hands in wet clay and sit at my potter's wheel. On the other hand, you rarely use the ether to explore the Other, so I suppose I'll take that for a win.

Naturally I appreciate the innumerable triumphs social media has garnered me. Casual cruelties, thoughtless lies, the endless sharing and repeating of the worst of yourselves, claiming it's "just a joke" when you're applauded and "ironic" when you're not. But it's honestly too cheap and easy a gain for me to enjoy. I'm feline like that — I prefer to play with my prey. When you fail to feel even the faintest tug of a dilemma, I lose interest in your path. I'm much too old to be entertained by the predictable.

But back to our girls.

"Are they still saying mean things to you on your phone?" Perdie ventured, finally.

"No," Rachel said sullenly, unconvincingly.

"What if I talked to the principal? To the bus driver?" Perdie had her own doubts about her suggestions. She didn't see how the adults could be oblivious to what was happening right under their noses. They must be wilfully ignoring it, maybe even silently sanctioning it as some kind of Darwinian approach to the social order. But what were her options? "If you tell me their names, I can try to talk to their parents."

"NO! God, Mom, are you crazy? Do you have any idea how

much worse my life would be if I wasn't just fat, I was a fat snitch? You're so ... dumb!"

Perdie grimaced. She couldn't argue with that. She didn't know when she'd felt so helpless. She'd managed to rescue her daughter from an abusive home, but she couldn't save her from a world cruel in its every inclination.

"Tell me what I can do." She couldn't help reaching for her daughter's hand, but she wasn't surprised when Rachel curled her fingers away.

"Nothing. There's nothing anyone can do. This is just my life. I'm the fat kid everybody hates."

Perdie's blood chilled at the despair in Rachel's voice. How could she tell her sweet, lovely daughter that this was only a few short years, that, after she graduated, she'd probably never see any of these kids again? That most of them would probably live wretched, pathetic lives while Rachel went on to create beautiful things and make genuine friends of authentic people? Perdie didn't know a way to say those things without discounting what Rachel felt right here, right now. How condescending and out of touch would that sound, when Rachel's whole existence in this moment was defined by the order of her classes and bus schedules and online notifications?

Perdie looked down and concentrated on regulating her breath so that her anger and, yes, hatred of those miserable little rats at school, wouldn't show in her face. She supposed that, as an adult, she should feel pity for them, too, because surely kids couldn't be so merciless unless someone had once been cruel to them, too; but she couldn't summon it up. They hurt her baby. She wished they were dead.

Aloud, she tried the only thing she had left.

"Baby, I love you so much. I wish you could see what I see — how completely, totally, wrong those fools are. You are beautiful, talented, kind, funny, smart. You're going to do amazing things in life. And you make our lives so much better by being here. Tad couldn't love you any more if you were his twin. Reilly adores you. Even Hannah would admit she thinks you're awesome if she were put to thumbscrews. Don't let those idiots at school define who you are."

"Okay, Mom."

Rachel didn't bother looking up, her glum rejoinder as good as telling Perdie to give it up. Perdie stood up and wrapped her arms around her stiff-limbed daughter, hugging her tight, as if she could infuse her with strength. "I'm going to fix dinner. Never doubt how much we need you."

"Sure."

Perdie's steps dragged as she walked back to the kitchen, where she stared blankly at the hamburger meat she'd taken out that morning and wondered what she was going to do with it.

How much of Rachel's vulnerability to this sort of abuse had been hardwired by her mother's own experiences? Matt had doted on the girls. Aside from that one frightening night in the hospital lobby, he'd never so much as raised his voice against them. But even with all Perdie's efforts to buffer them, there'd been times when they'd all witnessed his violence against her. Had that somehow built up a weakness in Rachel, a susceptibility to being a victim, to being prey, that the predators at her school had sniffed out? Had Perdie's acceptance of her own circumstances, even if only temporary, somehow taught Rachel that she was worth nothing more?

Perdie shook her head. There was no point pondering that now. It was too late to change the choices she'd already made. Maybe it went the other way. Maybe the uncertainty, the transience of their lives after fleeing Ohio, had been what set Rachel on her path to self-deprecation.

After all, both Rachel and Hannah had been completely secure in their father's affections before Perdie left. If she hadn't left, they'd have gotten to grow up with the friends they'd known since preschool. They wouldn't have had to adjust to multiple new schools, multiple new "homes". They wouldn't have had to experience economic insecurities. They'd have had a stay-at-home mom who went to school parties and scheduled playdates and chaperoned field trips and school dances. And Rachel's comfort eating hadn't started till the divorce, either. No matter how she looked at it, Perdie was to blame for Rachel's woes.

Now that's how I like to see someone. In my vast experience, the nearer you are to claiming responsibility for someone else's happiness or misery, the closer you are to me. Whether you admit it or not, every one of you has a God complex. To be fair, They kind of built it into you. At any rate, you'd all like to believe you have more control, more influence, than you do. That your choice, whatever it was, matters so much more than anyone else's. Which makes you easy to manipulate. Easy to drive to despair. And once in despair, you'll clutch at any unexpected lifeboat, however patently unseaworthy the craft.

Cheeseburgers and oven-baked fries, Perdie decided. Not exactly inspired, but no one would argue with it, either. She looked out the kitchen window, saw her husband and son hauling the last of the leaf bags to the curb. Had she been wrong all along, she wondered. Had all this happiness been entirely, selfishly, her own? Would her children always suffer just because she hadn't been willing to bear the consequences of her own choice when she married Matt? Maybe she'd been wrong. Maybe she'd only convinced herself that he would have eventually hurt Tad because she wanted so badly an excuse to get out on her own account.

And Reilly ... he was more than she'd ever deserved, anyway. He'd surely have found happiness without her.

Sometimes my job is so easy, it isn't any fun. Even a cat prefers to catch a mouse rather than have it stroll between its paws.

CHAPTER ELEVEN

Something had to change, Perdie thought a little desperately. She didn't know what or how. Every day Rachel came home wretched, and Tad came home angry. Perdie didn't know how long a child could live like that, isolated, bullied, hating herself.

But Rachel was more than a child, Perdie reminded herself. She was seventeen. Just another year and a half, and she could make her escape from the closed system of backbiting and gossip and cruelty that was high school. Surely, she could get Rachel through that amount of time. And maybe something would change. Maybe the bullies would get tired of Rachel and move on to some other poor soul. Maybe some of Tad's luck would rub off on her.

Perdie didn't know what it was, exactly, that charmed Tad's social status. He'd played a little baseball in elementary school, but his heart wasn't in it, and he hadn't had an interest in any other sports. He had a nice-looking face, shaggy blond hair that he wouldn't let her cut, and her own dark eyes. One day, he would grow into his skinny, over-long arms and legs and become a handsome man, but for now he was just a lanky kid. His love of science fiction, video games, and comic books should have landed him squarely in geek territory, but his bright humour and complete lack of self-consciousness allowed him to move seamlessly between all sorts of cliques. His grades could have been straight As but were mostly Bs because he'd rather talk than work. Even his teachers were as exasperated by him as they were fond of him, which could only be another point in his favour.

But Tad was two grades below his sister, in his first year at the county high school, while she was a junior. They shared no classes and had different lunch periods. His good social fortune couldn't help her.

Of course, you and I know the real reason everyone liked Tad. It was that light of his. Everyone has a light and a colour of their own, but most don't keep it. They hide it, they dim it, or they wind up so stained with all the ugliness and filth of this place that its hues change, sometimes permanently. But Tad was his light. If you'd ever suggested to him that he should change on account of someone else, that he should be less than what he felt, what he thought, what he imagined, he'd have looked at you in utter confusion. What comes as natural as breathing to most of you — subsummation of self to the will of the collective — was absolutely foreign to Tad. So when he moved through the world, he shone. And everyone wanted to stand a minute in that light. Not because it was fancy, or clever, but because it was unabashedly itself. And there's a peace in that, that you broken-up, scattered creatures crave.

But Perdie didn't know any of that. All she knew was that somehow or other, her son was afloat in the same sea that was drowning her daughter. So it wasn't that surprising when, come Wednesday night, she was adamant that Tad and Rachel should go to the dance together Friday night.

"Mom! I'm too old to go to a dumb school dance," Rachel protested. Tad merely arched his eyebrows at his mother and kept shovelling mashed potatoes into his mouth as if famine were imminent.

"I'm pretty sure the very fact that they have school dances means you are the exact age to attend one," Perdie returned, kicking Reilly under the table in an effort to solicit back-up. Reilly grimaced and shrugged, following Tad's lead in the vain hope that a full mouth would excuse him from speaking up.

Rachel rolled her eyes. "You know what I mean. It's going to be lame. Streamers and posters and Kool-Aid. I don't even know if any of my friends are going."

"I'm sure they'll go if they know you'll be there, too. And are you still going to claim that you're too old for school dances when the prom comes along?"

"Prom is different, obviously. For one thing, it won't be in a stinky school gym."

A second kick inspired Reilly to swallow and find his voice. "Maybe your mom's right. Maybe it will be fun. It's not like Jakob's Lake is exactly booming with other things to do this time of year. I mean, what are your other options? Playing Monopoly with me and your mom?"

Rachel huffed obstinately and snagged a dinner roll. "I'm sure Tad doesn't want to go."

Her brother shrugged. "I don't mind. Jake and Danny are going, and you know I'm a pretty bangin' dancer, so …"

Rachel paused in the middle of spreading butter and raised the roll threateningly. Tad threw up his hands in surrender.

"Kidding, kidding! I'm only a moderately good dancer. But I think we might as well go."

If they'd still lived in the city, Tad's interest in a school dance might have been surprising, but one of the drawbacks of living in a tiny mountain town was that many of their high school friends lived in other tiny towns, and school was their only chance to hang out. Neither of Tad's two new best friends lived in Jakob's Lake, so the school dance had a whole different appeal than it otherwise might.

"You could just play on the computer with Jake and Danny Friday night. That's probably what you're going to do all weekend, anyway," Rachel said scornfully.

"Except that Jake and Danny are going to the dance, so I can't play computer games with them Friday night," Tad returned reasonably.

Perdie sweetened the pot. "You could go to the thrift store after school tomorrow, maybe put together a new outfit. I could give you some money."

Rachel shook her head patronisingly at her mother, an elaborate eye roll thrown in for good measure. "That's not nearly enough time to design anything new. It's not as if I'd find anything that didn't need altering."

Rachel's outfits truly were creations, montages of fabrics and colours sewn together in unexpected but always beautiful ways. Privately, Perdie wondered if the real reason the other girls were so mean to Rachel was because they were jealous of her unique style, but she knew better than to voice that tired old cliché out loud.

"But I do have a new outfit I haven't worn yet."

"See?" Perdie tried and failed to keep the triumph out of her voice. "This is perfect. Tad can see his friends, and you have an occasion for your new dress."

"It's not a dress, Mom," Rachel said, shaking her head. "But okay. I guess we can go."

"I can teach you some new moves," Tad offered with a grin.

"Don't push your luck, or you'll lose your chauffeur," Rachel warned.

"Fine, fine. Just don't blame me when you embarrass yourself."

Later, when the teenagers had disappeared into their rooms, and Reilly was loading the dishwasher, Perdie leaned against the counter and regarded him thoughtfully. "I wonder if we should consider getting a second car."

Jakob's Lake was so small that, even with their cabin on the outskirts, they usually walked everywhere when the weather was good and often even once the snow had arrived. Perdie drove to her job at the Chamber of Commerce, which was on the opposite end of town where the highway went by, but Reilly had always been in the habit of walking to work. When they'd married, they'd sold both their vehicles and bought an SUV. Transportation was rarely an issue, as the car was mostly reserved for trips out of town or to the grocery store.

Reilly frowned, surprised. "Why?"

"If we had a second car, Rachel could drive herself and Tad to school instead of taking the bus. I know she has friends in some of her classes. I think the worst of the bullying takes place on those bus rides."

Reilly sighed, thinning his lips. *He's so handsome*, Perdie thought, thrilling to the flash of anger in his dark eyes, the set of his jaw. She knew his anger wasn't at her suggestion, but on Rachel's behalf, and that made her love him just a little more.

"I think if I could just get a few minutes to talk to those kids, I'd put the fear of God in them. I don't care if they like Rachel or not, I know I could convince them to sit down and shut up."

Perdie crossed the room and took his hand in both of hers.

"I know, honey, but she doesn't want us to help like that. She's absolutely certain it would only make things worse. Unbearably worse. And she's probably right. It's so tempting, but we can't sail in there and fight for her. Not like that."

"What makes them think they are so much better than her, anyway? So much prettier? Scrawny little things painted up like streetwalkers who probably will never make it to college —"

"Stop it," Perdie laughed, moving away as she shook her head. "Now you're just as bad as they are. We can't attack them in the same way they're attacking Rachel. We're the grown-ups. We have to be better than that."

Reilly shrugged, still visibly angry. "Maybe you do. They better not say anything where I can hear them, that's all I'm saying."

"Okay, okay." Perdie was still laughing. "But barring an all-out offensive on the schoolgirls, having her own ride to school might be the only thing we can do to help Rachel."

"I have two concerns with that. One, how would Hannah feel about that? We bought her a new bike when she went to school, but since she was living on campus, we didn't think she'd need a car. Now that she's off-campus and living in an apartment, she could probably really use a vehicle. And second, I don't know if I want Rachel driving all the way to the high school and back every day. There are a lot of accidents on that highway, and she's so young."

Perdie blew out a breath. "Well, that's all true. I do think Hannah would understand if we told her what Rachel is going through, and maybe Hannah needs to have a little bit of a hard time. I mean, if she's going to make this huge life change, she has to consider what it will cost."

"But at the same time, we can't punish her for choosing a life other than the one we anticipated for her," Reilly spoke gently. "And as the oldest, Hannah has always done a lot of understanding, a lot of accepting. Maybe more than is fair. I'd like to think about helping her, whether we agree with her or not."

Perdie looked down at her hands as if a better answer waited there. "That's true. Life hasn't been fair to these kids, and neither have I."

I don't think you have any idea what you people mean by "fair". Have you ever considered what life would look like if it were fair? And don't start spouting stuff about everyone having enough to eat and free healthcare and roofs over everyone's head. That might be what it would look like if life were idyllic, but we're talking fair here. Just. Equitable. If you always got exactly what you gave. You always say "life isn't fair" as if that were an unfortunate negative, but you forget how well I know you. If life were truly fair, you'd be a very unhappy lot of people.

Imagine if you received the same kindness and understanding you offered everyone else, and no more. If every time you snapped at someone, they snapped back. Every time you cut someone off in traffic, you got cut off, too. If everyone heard out loud all your secret mean thoughts. If you only received the same second chances and benefits of the doubt that you extended to others. One of the weirdest cruxes on which this whole strange universe spins is the imbalance of generosity. How a light like Anne Frank can shine undimmed through all the darkness of the Holocaust, how the stubborn illumination of a single Malala reveals the innumerable ugliness she has not the strength to banish. If the world were fair, we wouldn't even know their names. They'd be swallowed up in the tally. But somehow, their light burns far beyond the measure of their tiny wicks. Fair isn't all it's made out to be.

Now it was Reilly who crossed the room. Pulling Perdie

into a tight hug, he murmured against her hair. "You've always done everything you could. Nobody can be a perfect parent. Ours weren't. But they were good parents. Your kids know how much you love them, and that's all any of us can do. The rest we just muddle. Hannah is doing much better than you feel like she is right now. And Rachel is going to be okay. She has all of us, and she's going to get through these tough times. Everybody is going to be okay."

Perdie relaxed into his embrace, believing him because she wanted to so badly.

But that's the thing, isn't it? It's never going to be okay. Every one of your stories ends in grief. You know that adage? About how "everything will be okay in the end, and if it's not okay, it's not the end"? Perfect example of how beautifully easy it is for you to convince yourselves of a lie. The exact opposite is not only true, it's a truth played out thousands of times a day, printed for you in black and white on the obituary pages.

Oh, some of you will try to insist that the continuing existence of the soul hollows that bad ending of all its grief. Even your atheists try to find some beauty in death, some meaning in the return of the materials of man to his origin point. Some of you actually imagine comfort in the idea of recycling through the whole wretched drama again and again, meeting not one death, but endless deaths through time.

But all of that is bunk. Have you ever seen death yourself? There's nothing beautiful or peaceful about it. It's ugly, rotten, with a horror so insurmountable that you make movies and write books to try and coax it into a bearable familiarity, but you can't succeed. Have you ever watched the light go out of someone's eyes? If you have, you know that's a literal expression, not a poetic one. All the light, all the humanity ekes away into nothing and leaves a vacuous, gaping, stuffed sack of horror in its place. Those eyes don't glaze, they don't dim, they fill with a horrible, inhuman darkness.

Oh, and while we're on the subject, your pretty little head imagines a conclusion full of harps and angels and mostly just the idea of a world without this worst of enemies: death. You forget, though, that Death is an angel. Death is definitely going to be there, wherever there is. You'll have to make friends, that's all.

So whenever someone tells you that everything will be all right, that everything will be okay in the end, they're lying to you. It's not going to be okay. You will never be all right again.

That's why I'm here. To offer you some options. You might as well make the most out of this while you're here. You've been cheated, after all. The Creator crammed never-ending consciousness into a cloth bag, stitched with time. They tell you to feel the wind, taste the sea, but somehow give up those delights in the end. I'm telling you to dance with the wind, get drunk on the sea, and fight that old angel Death for as long as you possibly can, because there is no victory in death.

In death, there is only death.

CHAPTER TWELVE

Perdie lost Thursday. It would haunt her till the day she died, but there was no getting it back. She simply lost it.

Friday was diamond-bright, every angle a blade on which she bled again and again, but she never did remember that Thursday.

She must have gone to work. Reilly must have gone to work. Tad and Rachel must have gone to school, come home again. They'd have all eaten dinner together, but she couldn't remember a single bite. Try as she might, she couldn't picture their last meal together at all, couldn't remember what they talked about. If they'd laughed or fought. The sound of their voices. Who left the table first.

But she remembered Friday.

As usual, she'd hardly seen the kids till they were heading out the door to the bus stop. Perdie didn't know what sort of experiences led television writers to show parents up at dawn, whipping eggs or flipping pancakes, while kids hastily sat down to eat a full meal before school. First of all, it took every trick in the book to get both kids moving that early — if she'd ever let them sit down, she'd never get them moving again. And barely conscious, super-grumpy teenagers did not want to fill their bellies with heavy food. It was all she could do to throw a Pop-Tart or a granola bar at them as they headed out the door. Besides, if two working parents dirtied all the dishes for breakfast, how would they cook dinner that night? Nope, granola bars were as good as it was going to get in the Rodriguez household.

Hugs and kisses and scowls and a swirl of gusty, snowflake-flecked air, and Tad and Rachel were on their way. Reilly was next. Although his shop didn't open the doors till 10, he started his day at 8 so he could have some dedicated time to do the books and work on repairs without interruption from walk-in customers. Perdie would be the last one out and the last one home that evening.

She planned ahead, knowing at least Rachel would be too busy getting ready for the dance to want to wait for her mom and a sit-down meal. Rachel would be deeply entrenched: makeup, hair, who knew how many wardrobe changes before she felt confident enough to leave the house. Tad, though, would probably just brush his teeth and hair — if Perdie reminded him — and maybe, maybe, put on a different shirt. So Perdie chopped potatoes and onions and threw a soup together in the crockpot before she went to work, leaving a note propped beside it to let everyone know to serve themselves whenever they liked.

Although, in the moment, Perdie had been certain that convincing Rachel to go to the school dance had been the right thing, she was second-guessing herself as she backed the car down the drive and headed to work. What if she was setting her beautiful daughter up for failure? What if the same kids who made her life miserable on the bus targeted her at the dance? What if Rachel came home impossibly broken, unwilling to try ever again? What if, what if, what if.

Perdie, like many of you, spent almost as much time living in the what-ifs as she spent in the should-haves. It's baffling to me, when your hours are already so short, that you discard as many as you do in the trash-heap of what isn't. But this little quirk of yours plays well for my purposes. Self-doubt and recriminations, that tired old certainty that reality hinges solely on your choices, drive more of your decisions than you might imagine.

And Perdie, that classic iteration of the mother-martyr, who already believed that her decision to abandon one life and create another had quite literally saved her children, was unsurprisingly susceptible to this. And that's the kicker, of course — every now and then, reality actually does pivot on a single choice. Just often enough for me to convince you it always does.

So Perdie existed on the fulcrum of the scales she carried with her everywhere, weighing every choice and thought and motivation against the happiness and safety of those she loved. I prefer when you weigh your thoughts and choices against the particular pleasures and joys I offer you, obviously, but that whole selfless-love schtick Perdie tried hard to practice was an eccentricity I couldn't get around. Eventually, though, I figured out how to use even that to my own ends. But that comes later.

At least Rachel would have friends there. As soon as she'd reluctantly consented to attend, her next mission had been ensuring that as many of her friends as possible would go as well. Perdie knew her unspoken fears were Rachel's fears, too, and that the girl wanted to at least build up some sort of perimeter of friendship as a buffer against whatever ugliness lurked on the gym floor.

When Perdie arrived at the Chamber of Commerce's

cheery welcoming building, already decorated for the Christmas holidays, she quickly re-swept the walk and threw down a smattering of salt to prevent slips and falls. Later, she'd remember every application filed, every phone call, every jingle of the doorbells, and the sweep of winter's pale golden sun across the carpet as the hours sped away.

Just like that morning, she'd hardly seen either Tad or Rachel after she came home that evening. She'd taken a hot shower, scraped the last of the remaining potato soup into a bowl and topped it off with crackers, and sucked it down while listening to Reilly recount his day as he moved the laundry from the washer to the dryer.

Old Mrs Hitchcock had brought in her "broken" vacuum cleaner again. She brought it in about every three months, always so pleased with how Reilly managed to resurrect it from the dead and keep it functional. He'd long since given up on explaining that it wasn't broken. Mrs Hitchcock was that unlikely combination of clean-freak and cat lady, and Reilly had quickly recognised the vacuum cleaner simply needed a deep-cleaning of its own and a filter change. Most people would do that sort of thing themselves, but the eighty-seven-year-old's eyes had glazed over when Reilly began explaining what to unscrew and what to replace. So now he kept that model's filter stocked in the shop and charged her $20 every few months to restore the machine to working order.

"It's the least we can do," he'd explained to Perdie. "I mean, we don't want all those cats on the street, right? Seems a small price to pay."

"You're a softie," Perdie had laughed, her protest perfunctory. She was more than happy to let Mrs Hitchcock have all the cats. She was happy with Dandelion. In spite of his many disappointments, Dandelion remained convinced that whenever anyone went to the front door, they were going on a walk, and he always eagerly expressed his appreciation at being included with lots of wiggling leaps.

So when she heard the kids come clattering down the stairs to leave for the dance, Perdie had rushed to lock him up in the laundry room. She regretted that later, too: when griefs were added to griefs, she tallied Dandelion's stolen farewell as a heavy one. At the time, though, she hadn't wanted him to get dog hair on Rachel's outfit.

At least she'd thought to get photos. She snatched up her cell phone.

"Turn around, my beauties!" she sang out. "Tad, put your arm around your pretty sister."

Tad made the requisite and unconvincing protest but quickly acquiesced. For the hundredth time, Perdie reflected on how beautiful her children were. Tad was still just a promise of a man to come, his height as yet unfulfilled by the mass that would have made him an impressive figure one day, his shaggy hair falling over his strikingly angular face and deep brown eyes in a fashion that would have made any pop star jealous. Cradled in the crook of his arm, Rachel was his opposite, but equally remarkable: shockingly bright-blue eyes sparkled beneath a curtain of thick black lashes, off-set by pale skin and long, gleaming, chocolate-brown curls. The sapphire of her scarf and the tights that emerged beneath her short black skirt electrified the impact of her gaze, which Perdie was relieved to see alight with pleasure that she rarely saw in her daughter's eyes these days. It was only the blind vagary of high-school fashion that declared Rachel unworthy; by any other standard, she was a striking beauty.

If only, Perdie thought, she could outlive these teenage years and see herself clearly in the glass. As beset as she was with self-doubt, Rachel would not allow even her own fears to compromise her devotion to her art. In consequence, she was spared the mistake so many women make of trying to hide their size, to force their bodies into so-called popular styles clearly designed for women without curves. Instead, when she designed her clothes, she embraced the size that she was and worked with it, rather than against it. Perdie wished desperately that Rachel could actually believe objectively in her own sufficiency and not just for purposes of her sewing machine. Still, it was a start.

And right now, that devotion to her art meant that, while Rachel did not look any smaller than she actually was, she looked absolutely stunning at just that size. Perdie's heart swelled. With all her heart she hoped nothing tonight would happen to dim that bright joy she saw shining in her daughter's eyes, joy she'd almost thought extinguished forever.

Tad — Tad was himself. This dance was no triumph of art over life, no vital social opportunity for him, and he looked as relaxed and at home in his own skin as he always did. More than once Perdie had envied him that self-possession, wondering where it came from. Even as a successful adult out from under the thumb of an abusive partner, she still caught herself worrying about what the other parents would think, how the grocery store checker was evaluating her purchases, whether or not random passers-by were decrying her lousy parking skills. Tad had always tried his best at life and then — this was the strange part — assumed that his best would be good enough. He was that most mythical of creatures — a teenager (or for that matter, a human being) without a particle of angst.

"Okay, okay!" Perdie finally waved them to relax, slipping her cell phone into her pocket. "You two look wonderful. You're going to have so much fun. Give me a kiss goodbye."

"No way," Rachel told her mother firmly. "I just put on my lipstick."

"Well, I wasn't asking for a French kiss," Perdie returned huffily. "Give me your cheek. I'll kiss you."

Rolling her eyes, Rachel consented. Reilly settled for a quick hug around her shoulders, wisely careful not to touch her hair. Tad, on the other hand, seized his mother by the shoulders and planted a hearty kiss on her forehead.

"Some of us," he told Rachel in a mock-effeminate tone, "thought ahead and used our twenty-four-hour, non-smear lipstick."

Laughing, Reilly dodged and tried to avoid a similar fate, but Tad grabbed him and smacked a wet one on his forehead too.

"Ew!" Rachel returned, fighting for a haughty expression. "You said smear. You know I hate that word."

"Smear, smear, smear," chanted Tad predictably as Rachel grabbed for the car keys hanging on the hook near the door.

"Rachel," Reilly said, and his suddenly serious tone caught her attention. "Be careful out there. I think the roads are all mostly dry, but it's dark. Don't get in a hurry, and pay attention to your blind spots."

"Yes, dear," she told her stepfather patiently, swinging the keys in Tad's face. "Come on, punk. Let's go."

"Have fun!" Perdie waved from the front porch as they headed down the driveway. "I love you!"

They were talking to each other in lower tones she couldn't catch, both of them waving back absently over their shoulders. Perdie and Reilly stood in the cold and the dark, watching the headlights back away and then turn down the road toward the highway.

"Date night!" Reilly declared triumphantly as he closed the front door against the winter night.

"What?"

"Oh, come on! Don't tell me that getting me alone wasn't

always your ulterior motive in getting those two both out of the house at the same time?" Reilly affected a hurt expression. "I'm crushed."

Perdie laughed, punching her husband lightly in the arm. "Oh, sure," she rejoined. "I mean, of course. Obviously. That's all I've been thinking about."

"That's more like it," Reilly grinned, yanking her against him and nuzzling her neck. "It's good to be wanted."

THE ACCIDENT

CHAPTER THIRTEEN

Blearily, Perdie came to attention as her husband answered his phone. She pushed herself to a sitting position, pushed her hair behind her ears. The television was still on, but she'd dozed off there on the couch, snuggled against Reilly's warmth.

She had time to wonder if he'd been asleep, too. Time to wonder what time it was. Time to remember that they were waiting up on the couch because the kids were out. Time to realise that a phone call at one in the morning wasn't going to be good news.

Even in the blue illumination cast by the television screen, she could see her husband's normally olive complexion first pale and then flush a deep red as he listened to the voice on the other end. Cold suffused her limbs. Mindlessly, she began stroking her palms up and down her forearms, a futile attempt at a calm that wouldn't come again. She could feel rooms in her brain slamming shut their doors, throwing the locks, leaving her just one little space to breathe, one dark corner in a dark hallway to take and sort information and keep it safely away from the part of herself that would know what it meant. Her husband's words fell into that space, and coolly, carefully, she placed each syllable into a box just its size.

"How badly are you hurt?"

"How is your brother?"

"Where are you?"

"Was anyone else hurt?"

Before Reilly hung up the phone, Perdie had already slipped into her shoes and coat. She walked into the kitchen and pulled the cover off the doggie door so Dandelion could come and go at will. When she returned, arms draped with her purse and Reilly's coat and shoes, he was pacing by the front door. His right hand scrubbed repeatedly at his face, which contorted into a mask of agony that terrified her with its strangeness, smoothed back out, and contorted again.

Caught in the excruciation of ignorance, Perdie wanted to ask what had happened, but she couldn't make her lips conform to language. She was as afraid to make her husband say the words as she was afraid to hear them. Together, they walked into the frigid night air, awash in the glitter of the lightest of snows, and stared stupidly at the empty driveway.

"Justin. Justin," Perdie finally managed, slapping uselessly at Reilly's arm. He nodded, seemingly as voiceless as she, and they walked back inside as he dialled Justin's cell phone.

That was how Perdie heard what she already knew. She scarcely recognised Reilly's voice, strangled with tears and coarse with fiercely overlaid control, as he spoke.

"Rachel and Tad have been in an accident. They have the car. Can you drive us to the hospital?"

Thank God Justin hadn't wasted time on questions. That had been all he needed to know. Ten minutes later, it wasn't

Justin's pickup, but Alan's cruiser that pulled up in front of their house, blue lights blazing. Neither Perdie nor Reilly even recognised the novelty of sitting in the back of the cruiser behind the grate, as if they were criminals. The vehicle took off smoothly, its lights and markings allowing them to reach the county hospital far faster than they ever would have alone. It wouldn't be until weeks later that the radio silence in the car would register with Perdie, that she'd register the small, vital kindness of Alan turning down his communications before they got in the car. He wasn't on duty, so no harm was done.

On duty or not, it wasn't the Alan they knew in the driver's seat, though. It was Alan, the deputy sheriff, his calm, regular, professional tone just enough to keep hysteria at bay as he spoke soothingly. Perdie didn't know what he was saying, and she didn't know if Reilly knew either, but the coaxing rhythm of his speech nonetheless kept her mind from splintering apart as she clung to the shreds of her self-control. Justin sat silent in the passenger seat, his presence a stony comfort that could offer no lies.

Perdie's phone buzzed against her pocket, and she withdrew it shakily, staring at the display.

"It's a blocked number," she managed finally.

"Don't answer it," Alan said swiftly, firmly.

"What? I have to. It might be—"

"It's not. That will be the Highway Patrol trying to reach you. We're already on our way. We'll be there in fifteen minutes. Nothing they can tell you will make this better."

If she'd been thinking clearly, she'd have recognised the ominous import of those words, but in the moment, all she felt was a rush of relief at being told not to answer the phone. Terror constricted her veins, her throat, making it hard to focus, hard to breathe. How could she do something as mundane as say hello to a stranger, then listen to them tell her something terrible she already knew?

But she didn't know. Not yet.

Her husband seemed at least as tortured as she was. He had curled in almost entirely on himself, his fists clenching and unclenching on his knees. She could see his cheek flexing as his jaw tightened and fixed. He stared straight ahead, and Perdie had a sudden, compelling vision of him surrounded by a wall of flames, black, choking dust swirling around his head, his skin blackening and curling off the bones, and all the while his gaze fixed, fixed on a tableau she couldn't see.

He'd guessed, you see.

Rachel had said just enough, seen just enough, that he realised what even his stepdaughter hadn't known to be true. And now he was separate from her — alone with truth. He could have spilled out his fears, told his wife what he imagined to be true, could have plunged her into that awful fire along with him. But some part of his mind recognised that she had just a few minutes more to be the mother of three children, and he couldn't bring himself to take those few minutes away from her.

Alan and Justin knew, too. In the handful of minutes it had taken to reach the Rodriguez house, Alan had made a call, identified himself, learned the worst. But years of experience had taught Alan that there is an important order of operations to be followed. You have to allow people to go through the motions, accept one piece of information at a time. Get to a safe place. See a uniform.

Death is easier when it's official.

Never, ever underestimate ritual. Sometimes ritual is all that stands between the mortal mind and madness.

So Alan and Justin hid their own tears and left Reilly alone, untouched, in his knowledge, and left Perdie outside of her own.

CHAPTER FOURTEEN

I watched them come through the ER doors with avid interest.

That's where I was waiting, you see. Finally, we come to the crux of the thing.

I was as nondescript as I could be. I might have been white, I might have been Hispanic, I might have been Native, I might have been Asian. I was certainly female and certainly old, wrapped in a less-than-fresh collection of sweaters and scarfs and holey gloves, with a thin halo of silvery hair.

I know it's very evil-witch-in-the-woods, but the trope exists for a reason. Fairly or not, old women are rarely feared and often heeded and you certainly don't recognise them as potential threats. So the costume is a useful one. I get tired of it, sometimes, but it's too effective a guise to drop. It would still be a while before Perdie noticed me, though.

Reilly and Perdie remained very much alone as they came through those doors. Even the closest friend stands miles away from the stricken parent in the hour of bereavement. Alan and Justin were one in their shared understanding of the facts, few as they were. Social mores about the stoicism of men are the merest of useless props when faced with real life and real loss. Still, for the Rodriguez' sake, Alan and Justin fought to keep their own sorrow at bay, borne down not just by the loss, but by the fear and grief of their friends. More than once they swept at their eyes. Alan's unfortunate breadth of experience with death might have made this easier for him, but the opposite was true; after all, he knew better than any of them what was coming, how bad it would get.

Reilly's haunted gaze moved endlessly around the room. He was afraid to look at his wife, afraid she'd see the truth in his eyes.

Perdie was in full mom-mode, focused on what needed to be done and needing badly to believe that whatever it was, she could do it. But Alan swept her behind him, forcing her into Reilly's accidental, reflexive embrace, as Alan went to the desk and exchanged a few low words with the woman seated there. His badge flashed.

She nodded, pressed a button, and the security doors to the ER opened. Alan turned back to the others.

"Right this way. You guys have a few minutes to talk to Rachel before they take her into surgery. Justin and I will be right outside the door, okay?"

"Surgery?" Perdie clutched at Reilly's arm, stumbled as they hurried to follow Alan down the hallway.

"I'm sure the doctor will explain when we get there. They'll need your consent."

"Tad. Tad," Perdie managed to get her son's name out, but that was as close as she could get to asking the question.

"Right now, Rachel is the priority," Alan told her gently, and, mistaking his meaning, Perdie felt a great swell of relief.

Parents are never prepared to see their children hurt. Perdie and Reilly both gaped and gasped like beached fish when they pushed past the curtains, registering the cuts and abrasions, the swelling flesh. Rachel's face was scarcely recognisable, one side badly distorted and already blackening, her eye closed. Cursory efforts at cleaning her up had only been intended to clear the wounds, and her hair was stiff with blood. Perdie reached for her then drew back, unsure where she could touch her that wouldn't hurt. Finally, she lifted a hank of Rachel's hair, flinched at the spider-webbed glass caught there. Reilly went around to the side where Rachel's one open eye, its white completely red, filled with tears.

"It's okay, honey," he said soothingly, stroking her arm. "It's okay. You're going to be okay."

There you go again. But it's not okay. It's not going to be okay. Still, that reassurance which no one believes is always the first thing out of your mouths.

"Tad," Rachel whispered. Perdie's hand went to Rachel's mouth but stopped short, as if she wanted to soothe the cracked, swollen lips.

"He's okay," Perdie said urgently, not knowing otherwise. "He's okay. You're going to be okay, too, baby. We just need to talk to the doctor, and they're going to fix you up."

"Mr and Mrs Rodriguez?" The doctor appeared behind them, no doubt summoned by the nurse as soon as they'd gotten word the parents were here. He had a clipboard and a pen in his hand.

Perdie couldn't bring herself to leave Rachel, even for the doctor, so she stood at the bottom of Rachel's bed with her hand resting on her daughter's sock-clad foot under the sheets and tried to force her eyes to remain focused on the doctor's face as he explained the procedures in a low voice. *Something is wrong with my eyes*, Perdie thought. They kept bouncing around the room, fixing on random articles for an instant, then bouncing away again. Her upper lip twitched, and she sucked her lips in between her teeth. Even the doctor's words seemed to be bouncing, rattling around in her head and refusing to stay in the order they were spoken.

When the doctor extended the clipboard, Perdie signed it, hardly knowing why, and the doctor immediately motioned to a couple of nurses standing by. They bustled past, snapping up the rail guards on Rachel's bed, unlocking the wheels. They were taking her away, Perdie realised dimly, wondering why it seemed so dark in here when the fluorescent lights couldn't possibly be any brighter.

"Good night, baby," she said inanely, pressing the softest kiss she could to Rachel's protruding cheek. "You'll be back soon."

Reilly bent and pressed a kiss in his stepdaughter's palm, wrapping her fingers around it. Her bruised and bloodied fingers clutched spasmodically at the ephemeral token.

"Don't worry," one of the nurses said firmly. "We'll take good care of her and have her back before you know it."

Reilly came around and wrapped an arm around Perdie's shoulders, clutching her close as they watched Rachel disappear down the hallway. It seemed like an eternity since she'd felt her husband's warm, solid strength against her, and for a brief second, Perdie nearly allowed herself to collapse into him. But then she straightened, snapping her spine erect and shrugging out from beneath his arm. She grabbed his clammy hand instead.

"Tad," she said, her gaze skating away from the lines and bagging skin on her husband's face. Something terrible had happened to Reilly, she thought. He looked like Rip Van Winkle must have looked, as if he'd aged a hundred years since the last time she saw him in the light.

"Tad," he echoed, and the hopeless helplessness in his voice sent alarms jangling through Perdie.

"Reilly?" she asked.

He didn't answer, just tugged on her hand and pulled her toward the nurse's station.

When the woman there looked up, he managed, "We have another child here who was in the same accident. Tad Rodriguez. I mean — Tad Blevins."

The nurse's lips tightened as she tried to keep the pity from washing over her face. "Let me get the doctor for you."

This doctor was a woman, with tired eyes and grey-streaked hair. Perdie was grateful for the little differences, the small details she could set her brain to cataloguing. No wedding ring, she noticed, and wondered if most doctors didn't wear wedding rings so they didn't have to risk losing them in a bin of medical waste every time they stripped off their gloves.

"Follow me," the doctor said, leading them to a small, quiet room with soft chairs, lamps instead of bare bulbs, a door that closed.

Perdie looked longingly at the door as it clicked softly shut, somehow knowing that she would never really be on the other side of that door again.

"Have a seat, please," the doctor said.

Perdie was already shaking her head as she lowered herself into the chair, suddenly aware that her knees wouldn't have held her up any longer anyway.

But denying the truth could not delay it any longer.

"I'm very sorry," the doctor said. Perdie was sure, afterward, that the doctor had told them her name, had almost certainly introduced herself as soon as she'd approached them, but it had slipped away, one more meaningless sound in a sea of sounds that only said one thing, in the end.

"Your son Tad is dead. We tried to save him, but his injuries were too severe. There was nothing we could do."

Beside her, Reilly dropped his head into his hands and sobbed, an ugly, frightening, soundless weeping that felt like an earthquake.

The doctor must still have been talking, because her voice rumbled over Perdie's consciousness like musical notes, but the only words that Perdie could hear were her own.

"Nonononono..."

The white mass with the voice moved out of Perdie's vision, and distantly she heard the door closing again. Numbly, frantically, she fell to her knees and began scrabbling to get under the chair, against the wall, the rough, short carpet scraping her arms, as if there were some way to crawl out of this reality, as if she could dig out of the hospital, out of the truth. When her head hit the wall, the wail cut itself out of her, clawing its way up from her womb, through her raw throat, out her open mouth. Her fingers pulled at the edges of her mouth, as if there were a way to empty herself of pain.

But every exhalation only made room for more pain. All those doors she'd slammed so securely shut in her mind flung themselves open, and still the house of pain that was her body was not big enough. Her foundations crumbled; her walls dissolved.

It might have been a few minutes, it might have been a year, before her husband's gentle hand on her back registered. Slowly, Perdie came back into her skin, and, oh God, it was such old, old, broken skin. Reilly lifted the chair off of her, reaching under her arms and pulling her up, into another chair. *My bones*, she thought, *my bones are brittle*. She felt made of paper, awash in a storm. Reilly sank to his knees at her feet, resting his head in her lap. Her hands — useless hands — lay on his head, absently stroking his hair. He remained there only a moment before standing, brushing himself down as if he were rumpled rather than heartbroken.

"Let me identify him," he said in a low voice she hardly recognised.

Those words propelled her up. "No," she said fiercely. "I need to see him. I need to see my baby."

Reilly gripped her by the forearms and spoke firmly. "No, you don't. Not like this. This isn't anything you want to see. Let me do this. You can see him later. After they ... clean him up."

Something in his tone must have gotten through to her, because she shrank away from his touch as she relented. "Wait here for me," Reilly said. "The police are out there. I don't want you to talk to them alone."

"The police?"

"Yes. I'll — I'll bring back some coffee. We'll talk to them together."

She didn't watch Reilly through the window in the door that closed behind him. She didn't want to think about the world outside this room. In that world, her son was dead. In that world, her daughter was in surgery. In that world, the police were waiting for her. Somewhere, a mortician was waiting for her. A gravedigger.

She supposed she should pray. She had nowhere else to turn, no one else to appeal to for help. But prayer required words. She had to know what to ask for. She had to know what had happened. And all she knew right now was this nameless, featureless, colourless void growing inside of her.

This couldn't be real, she thought helplessly. It can't be. Her mind played those last minutes before the kids left the house that night, over and over again. She kept seeing that one too-long lock of dusky-blond hair falling into Tad's eyes, the laughter in his face. She wanted to push it back, wanted to frame his face in her hands, feel his mobile strength under her hands, smell that warm-boy scent when she hugged his neck. Blindly, she lifted her hand, pressed her fingers to the spot on her own forehead where he'd pressed that silly, sloppy kiss.

Last kiss.

This couldn't be real.

She fixed her eyes on the wallpaper and began counting the knots winding their way floor to ceiling.

CHAPTER FIFTEEN

When Reilly came back through that door, two steaming paper cups in his hands, he was a different man. Even Perdie, lost in her grief, could see that she was no longer married to the same man who'd told her to wait for him in this room.

It would be a while before Rachel came round from her anaesthesia, longer still before her mind unmuddied and reordered the night's events sufficiently for her to explain what seemed inexplicable just now. Eventually, what emerged as a reason was the flimsiest of hooks on which to hang a life.

Honestly, most of them are. You always want reasons, explanations, causes, someone to blame. When you can't find them, you make them up. You simply can't accept that something so precious to you can be stolen in an instant, with no effort at all. But it can. It regularly is. So it was here.

Tad's cell phone had slid out of his pocket and into the floorboard of the passenger seat behind him. So, he'd unbuckled — just for a second — and clambered over the seat to grab his phone.

It was dark. On a country road. Distracted by her brother's acrobatics, Rachel didn't see the unlit stop sign, didn't see the headlights obscured by an outcropping of pine trees at the intersection.

So, when all the vagaries and coincidences that created Rachel's particular trajectory that night collided with all the vagaries and coincidences of a stranger's, when they crossed by mere millimetres, when they overlapped by less than a second's shared space on a Venn diagram, when all of this happened, Tad wasn't wearing his seatbelt.

Instead, he was propelled through the windshield at a terrific rate of speed, across the back of the other car, and into the cold, wet field on the other side of the road.

And when the two vehicles finally stopped their mad, tangled dance in that field too, Tad was underneath them.

Mostly underneath them, anyway. He didn't know it; a small kindness, I suppose. His heart did, though, and it wasn't quite ready to give up even then. It had hung on, thumping in fits and starts, unwilling to stop.

What a light that was. Even I had to stop and watch it go.

The EMTs didn't see it, of course. You are so frightfully limited in what you can apprehend, even here in this plane created entirely for you. But it filled that field, a starburst of colour and brilliant warmth that soothed even my restless limbs, just for a moment.

And then it was gone.

Light seeks light, without hesitation, without prevarication, without explanation. It simply does. Tad found his way home as if he'd never been lost.

But the ones left behind are always a different story.

Reilly didn't get to see the light, after all — just all the darkness left in its wake.

The Reilly who wrapped his wife in his arms now was a different man from the one he had ever been before. For the rest of his life, no matter how fiercely he wished otherwise, he would always remember Tad as he'd last seen him —as a crumpled, broken, empty thing, a smashed pile of bones and shredded flesh. He'd been right not to let Perdie go, and forever grateful that she'd never know what that gift had been.

For now, he hugged his wife and wished her warmth could banish this cold that had found its way into his veins.

"Coffee," he said, and gratefully she took the cup from him, lifted it to her lips. It wasn't so much that she was tired, even though by now they were well into wee hours. It was one of those rituals that provides so much comfort. She didn't know how to be a mother to a dead child, but she did know how to pretend that coffee could clear her foggy mind and strengthen her shaking limbs. So, she did that instead.

"Rachel?" she asked.

Reilly shook his head. "Not yet. But we should talk to the police."

"Yes, the police," Perdie agreed dully.

Together they left the small room and re-entered the real world, where sounds and lights and rushing feet surged around them. Alan and Justin were still where they had left them, though the coffee cups in both their hands attested to their same reliance on ritual. A third man, his uniform identifying him as Colorado State Patrol, was speaking to them in a low voice, his face grave but not unkind.

Alan saw their approach and broke off, waving them over.

"This is Perdie Rodriguez," Alan said, and Perdie realised

that Reilly must have already met the officer when he'd had to identify their son. "Perdie, this is Trooper Milliken."

The man extended a big hand that enfolded hers as gently as if she were made of glass.

"Ma'am," he said, and Perdie felt a new rush of tears threatening at the sympathy in his voice. "I'm so sorry for your loss. I tried to speak to your daughter before she went into surgery, but she was still shook-up and pretty confused. Do you mind if I ask you a few questions?"

"Questions?"

Alan laid a hand on her shoulder. "He has to fill out a report, Perdie. There'll be an investigation."

"Investigation? Oh, God. Was there ... there was another driver? She didn't just go off the road? Is anyone else hurt?"

Perdie had been so focused on her children, she hadn't even considered the possibility that the whole truth could be even worse than she already knew.

"There was another driver, ma'am," Trooper Milliken told her. Somehow, she took strength from the steadiness of his dark eyes. She sensed that he would tell her the truth, however bad it might be, and that was oddly reassuring. "That person is here at the hospital, too, but I don't believe their injuries are life-threatening. I can't be sure, but I don't believe your daughter's vehicle struck the front of the other car directly."

"Struck the other car? It was her fault?"

"That's one of the things we have to determine. Right now, we've got a couple of smashed cars in the dark and a couple of confused drivers. So, we have to ask a lot of questions, do some reconstructing, try to understand what happened."

"And if it was Rachel's fault? What happens then?" Her mother-brain was racing, eager for any new disaster on which it could seize, any new problem it could solve that wasn't choosing a coffin or writing a eulogy.

The trooper shrugged, his lips twisting as he settled his hands on the belt at his ample waist. "It's hard to say, ma'am. It depends on the circumstances. Could be a citation. Could be a suspension. Could be criminal charges."

Unthinkingly, Perdie clutched at his arm. "Charges? But she's hurt. Her brother is dead."

Alan stepped between Perdie and the trooper, gently unfolding her fingers from the other man's arm. "Justin, why don't you stay here with Reilly and Trooper Milliken? Perdie, come for a walk with me."

Justin, his drawn features nearly as exhausted as Reilly's, nodded. "We'll be here."

Reilly still hadn't said a word.

Alan put his arm around Perdie's shoulders and drew her down the hall. He didn't speak till they got clear of the ER doors and into the relative quiet of the waiting room. There, he refilled her coffee cup and sat beside her in the hard, plastic chairs.

"Perdie, there are very few questions you can answer for the trooper. You weren't there. You might guess, but you don't know what happened. You don't know what the kids did or didn't do at the dance. To be totally fair, you don't even know if they went to the dance."

"Of course I do," Perdie protested, baffled as to why Alan was talking like this. "What do you mean?"

"I mean the only questions you can answer are questions of which you have direct knowledge. You know what happened at your house before the kids left, and that's all. Even then, you don't know what the kids were doing in their rooms before they left."

"Alan, I don't know what you're talking about. What would they have done?" Comprehension flashed through her, and rage was its quick cousin. "I know you're not suggesting they

124

were high or drunk. You know my kids, Alan. You know they'd never do that."

"Shh, shh," Alan cautioned her, patting her knee.

Angrily, she brushed it aside.

"Perdie, kids do all kinds of dumb things for all kinds of dumb reasons. Of course, I know that neither one of them would do those things — ordinarily. But you and I don't know if it was an ordinary night. We don't know anything besides what time they left the house and what they were wearing, what they were driving."

"Why are you talking like this, Alan? How can we even think about this right now when … when …" Her voice broke, subsided.

"I'm talking like this because we need to look out for Rachel right now. We don't have any idea what happened tonight. But we know the other driver has been injured, and we know that Tad is dead. That means Rachel could potentially be looking at serious charges, even vehicular homicide charges. So, say only what you absolutely know and stick to the facts. And it wouldn't be a bad idea to have an attorney for when Rachel wakes up, before she's interviewed again by the police."

Panic swamped Perdie. "Reilly — what if Reilly says something?"

Alan shook his head. "Justin won't let Reilly say anything he shouldn't. Milliken isn't looking to get Rachel in trouble, but he has to be objectively on the side of the law, and in this case, that means on Tad's side. If this accident turns out to be Rachel's fault, then she could be charged for his death."

Even as they left his mouth, Alan's words took on a surreal horror. Was there some world, some legal definition, that would require Perdie to consider her daughter her son's murderer? An image of the two of them as she'd last seen them, framed in her phone camera, flashed through Perdie's mind. Was she supposed to feel angry at Rachel? Resentful? Was she somehow betraying Tad if she didn't? She could only save the child still breathing, but did that mean she was abandoning the child lying cold and airless on a steel bed somewhere in this horrible place?

Too many questions. Too many impossibilities thrust into her hands.

She tried to do what she could.

"But he's her brother. She doesn't even know yet ..." Perdie's voice wavered, but she swallowed and went on. "She'll be destroyed. How could they charge her?"

"Maybe they won't. But the law doesn't care who you are, Perdie. It only cares what you've done. So, when we go back there, say as little as you can. Get a lawyer. Take care of Rachel."

Perdie nodded, twisting her fingers over and over in her lap. *This is how people go mad*, she thought. She didn't know if she could absorb one more fact, one more piece of information.

"I need — I need a minute," she murmured softly. "Just a minute."

Alan nodded. "That's okay. We'll be waiting for you when you're ready."

She stared after his back as he headed out the ER doors. Slowly, she got to her feet, moving to the front doors of the hospital like a stoop-shouldered old woman.

I had been waiting for her there, in the lobby. I had watched, fascinated by the interplay of emotions across their faces, fascinated by the emotions they buried under the skin. I'd worked so hard to get her alone, but in the end, Perdie built her own solitude. Grief has a way of doing that. When most of you need community to survive, you withdraw, retreat, like a dumb beast who prefers to die untouched rather than wrapped in the solace of those who loved it. Even in that forlornness, though, you hope for something, some comfort, some answer. And I am a marvellous peddler of somethings.

I gave her a moment to draw a cool, crisp breath under the parking lot lights before I walked out to join her.

CHAPTER SIXTEEN

For all your pretensions about individualism, independence, introversion, and the like, you are — every one of you — a herd animal. Even when you imagine you're seeking solitude, you're really looking for one particular person. You may not want the whole herd, but you do want that one other animal who smells like home, who can understand you without more than a comforting nicker passing between you. You want help.

I leaned up against the curb stop a few feet away from Perdie.

"You don't look all right, dear," I said, relying on my quavery voice to signal compassion rather than nosiness.

"I'm not all right," responded Perdie in a dull voice.

I probably could have appeared as a mountain goat, and she'd have answered the same. She'd lost the ability to question or examine any more of her circumstances.

"I've made a terrible mistake."

"I reckon we've all made terrible mistakes."

Perdie tipped her head back, almost as if she'd lost the

strength to hold it up, and gazed out on the heavy, bright stars hanging out of reach of the parking lot lights.

"Not like this. I wish to God I'd never left."

"Left?"

"I did this. I did all of this."

"I'm sure that's not right," I offered, hoping to convince her of the opposite.

It's amazing how easy it is to persuade you that your choices are the only ones that really matter in the end. Your longing after relevance trips you up every time.

"It is, though. I was so selfish. If only I'd stayed."

"Stayed?"

"Stayed. In Ohio." Perdie swung to face me, almost as if realising for the first time that she wasn't speaking to herself.

"I'm sure you had good reasons for leaving."

She cocked her head as if examining me, registering my withered face and heaps of dirty clothes; but she was only measuring her own choices in her head.

"I thought so, but then, I *wanted* to think so. I *wanted* to believe that I had to leave so that I could. It wouldn't have been enough to leave because I wanted to. Because I was scared for myself."

"Sounds like a good reason to me."

"It wasn't, though. Not when it brought us here. If I'd stayed, my son would still be alive. If I'd stayed, my daughter wouldn't be under the knife, waking up only to be under arrest — maybe under arrest. If I'd stayed, Hannah wouldn't be throwing her life away on a whim."

I watched her pluck spasmodically at her trousers.

"How can you be sure?"

"Everything happens for a reason, right? And tonight is the

sum of all my choices. If I'd stayed in Ohio, I'd have been at home for them." The pitch of her voice rose. "I could've helped them so much more. Could have seen when there was trouble. Hannah wouldn't have been so cut-off and angry all the time. Poor Rachel wouldn't have been so sad and insecure. And Tad — Tad would have a chance." Her voice cracked. "Tad would be here." She sucked in a panicky, sob-rattled breath before subsiding into a stillness that was downright eerie, even to me.

Everything happens for a reason. Quite possibly the best lie I ever told. What I really love is when people attribute it to God, as they nearly always do.

I mean, seriously. Are you kidding me? "Everything happens for a reason?" What reason would that be? You can't cling to this lovely notion of free will and still think that God is micro-managing every falling leaf and crashing car. The reason the vast majority of "things happen" is selfishness, pure and simple.

It's not that God doesn't care: of course They do. I wish They cared less. But They can't let you be remotely human if They're going to interfere every time you make a decision.

And your decisions aren't the only ones — or even the biggest ones — at play, of course. There wouldn't be much point in designing a vastly complicated, highly organised system of protons, neutrons, and electrons, of tides and tremors, of day and night, if They intended to string every cell together by hand, every millisecond of every minute. What would be the point? It would be rather like creating a complex AI to play ping-pong against, and then insisting on running back and forth like a madman from one side of the court to the other, lobbing every ball back and forth against yourself. Not only preposterous as an attempt at a game, but there's no chance of a victory when you play like that.

But these aren't arguments I make out loud, of course. I can only be grateful when you swallow the fiction whole.

"You'd give it all up, huh?"

"Every minute," Perdie rejoined fiercely, her hands balling into fists at her side. "I'd give up every minute of freedom, every minute of happiness, if I could just go back and stay."

"Give up your husband?"

It was a testament to Perdie's state of mind that she never questioned how I knew she had a husband, or why I was pursuing such an intimate line of questioning. She was looking for an angel that night, and she wasn't about to protest when she'd found one. The fact that my wings were darker than most was irrelevant at the moment.

"Yes." Her voice was low but unhesitating.

A mother's love is a raw and dangerous thing. Given the chance, it will devour everyone in its path, without hesitation or remorse. In my experience, men suffer much more agony over a choice between mother and child than any woman suffers over a similar choice between father and child. Women don't even register the dilemma. The child simply wins, while men torment themselves the rest of their lives over their decision, whichever way they go in the end.

"He'd be fine," she went on, dismissing Reilly's fate as if she'd never held it in her hands. "And he'd understand, if he knew. He'd want Tad to live."

That's not the choice I was offering, but how she perceived the distinction was on her, not me.

One more time, just to clarify.

"If there was a way to go back, to stay in Ohio, to have never left your first husband, to stay at home with your children, you'd do that?"

She looked me right in the eyes then. Looked at me and saw me, for the first time since she'd come outside. And that's when I saw the same woman who'd once fled Ohio without a single prospect, a fierce, fearless mother-goddess intent on one thing: saving her children.

A raw and dangerous thing.

"You'd give up everything you have here? Give up the person you've become? Give up your husband? Give up who your children are today?"

"Yes."

That was all I needed.

The stars spun away.

BEFORE THE ACCIDENT
TAKE TWO

CHAPTER SEVENTEEN

"You're a lifesaver!"

Perdie laughed, then winced at the mechanical sound. Julie didn't seem to notice, though. Perdie supposed the distance abetted by cell phones must provide some cover. "Don't worry about it. You'd do the same for me in a heartbeat. It's just a ride home from school."

"That's the thing," Julie said, sounding harried. "You know I wouldn't. I can't. I'm useless as a friend since the divorce. It's all I can do to get us all back and forth to work and school, and sometimes I can't even do that."

"You're a terrific friend," Perdie reassured Julie.

A year ago, Julie's husband Darren had filed for divorce, citing irreconcilable difference. The biggest difference had been his overly available co-worker Keri Bennett, who'd promptly dumped him as soon as the papers were finalised. Julie had gone back to work teaching, but she'd had to take a job with a district out of town, and her kids hadn't adjusted that well, between their dad walking away and their mom no longer being available 24/7 as cook, chauffeur, and general housemaid. When Darren came crawling back, claiming he was so sorry and had been "out of his mind," Julie's kids had been astounded and irate when their mother hadn't budged.

"There's nothing easy about what you're going through, and you're doing the best you can. That's all anybody can do."

"I'd love it if you could convince Lexie and Travis of that."

"Oh, no. I don't claim to be able to convince teenagers of anything. You're just going to have to wait for them to grow up and realise you were the best mom ever."

Julie snorted. "I won't hold my breath for that one. I better go, Perdie. Thank you so much for picking up Travis after practice."

"No worries."

But Perdie was worried. Luckily, Julie had called early in the morning, so Perdie could adjust her schedule and still have supper ready and the kitchen cleaned up by the usual time. Matt wouldn't be pleased about her leaving the house again after he was home: he expected all the errands and chores to be completed while he was at work, but hopefully he'd understand this was an unusual case. Normally Julie could make it to Travis' practice after she left work, but today she had some kind of parent-conference meeting that was scheduled to run long.

And there were some things Perdie could do to improve her odds. She'd planned on cleaning out the gutters today, getting the last of the autumn leaves out before the winter snows began in earnest, but she could leave that till tomorrow. Instead, she'd make the sure the interior of the house was sparkling, get all the clothes in the hampers washed. Oh, and she'd bake some of Matt's favourite rye bread. That was bound to put him in a better mood. It was just one little errand. Thirty minutes round-trip, no more. Now, if only she could count on the kids to be in good moods tonight, too.

Perdie felt downright out of breath by the time they started wandering in the front door that afternoon. She'd barely managed to get a shower and blow-dry her hair before Rachel made it home. The high school released first, and Tad would be next, about half an hour later. It wasn't that Matt expected her to be all gussied up on his account; if anything, the opposite was true. He'd have been suspicious if she looked too nice or put on make-up. But he did expect her to be clean, and he was always exasperated if he walked into the bathroom and found the mirror fogged or the floor damp. So, she'd learned long ago to manage her hygiene out of sight. Happily, the children had their own bathroom where Matt never stepped foot. *Now that room was a disaster of the first order*, thought Perdie. A teenage girl and boy sharing a mirror? Horror story fodder.

Rachel's entrance did not bode well for the evening.

Perdie heard the door slam and hurried to intercept her seventeen-year-old daughter before she could disappear into the vortex of her bedroom.

That's right — seventeen. Or haven't you figured out where we are yet? I offered Perdie the chance to have never left Matt, to have never left Ohio. It's the same week of the same year, relived as if she'd stayed.

All gifts come with caveats, though.

Perdie doesn't know she's living in a second chance. Everything and every memory about the life she chose before — Jakob's Lake, Reilly, even good old Dandelion — is gone. And of course, most importantly, all recollections of the accident itself are gone, too.

Maybe you think that's not fair. Maybe you think it's wrong to expect her to be able to make a choice about possibilities when she has no idea what the outcome of those possibilities may be. But now you're thinking like Perdie.

Perdie thought that her choices were the only ones that mattered in the end — that somehow, if she'd just been good enough, unselfish enough, smart enough, tough enough, she could have saved her children from that heartache and horror. She couldn't have, though. Heartache and horror are the defining characteristics of the human condition. It's possible that any number of different choices by Perdie could have prevented the accident. It's possible that a hundred different universes would have still converged on that single point. But some heartache and horror would have found them, sometime, somehow.

And the fundamental humour of the whole situation lies in your perpetual crawling and grasping after the impossible. You simply can't make the world run as you like. If you could, you wouldn't be human, you'd be God. And if you hadn't noticed, even They find that whole supreme-control bit tiresome in the extreme. It's great for building walls out of Legos or some such, but if you want actual relationships, interaction, emotion, you're going to have to allow for possibility and chaos and disaster. And yes, loss. Yet you always want it both ways.

Perdie would have wanted it both ways, too, if she could have dictated as much. But that wasn't the game we were playing. She had to make this choice blind — as everyone does. Even me. After all, I didn't know which way she was going to swing this time. Maybe she'd been right. Maybe this set of possibilities was not so awful as she'd imagined it, back ten years ago. Maybe Tad would make it to fifteen. Even sixteen. Maybe sixty-five.

See, I'm not so bad. No horns, no pointy red tail. I'm more like the author of one of those Choose-Your-Own-Adventure books. It's not my fault if you keep getting eaten by cannibals or falling into quicksand. There is a way out, after all. Whether or not you take it is always, entirely, up to you. I'm nothing more than a signpost. You like to blame me because I point in both directions, but you're the one who decides which way to go.

"Rachel!" Perdie grabbed her daughter in a quick hug, too accustomed to Rachel's instinctive stiffening to count it an affront. Still a couple of inches shorter than her mother and unlikely to make up the height, Rachel felt like a kitten in Perdie's arms, an unwieldy bundle of tiny bones and soft skin. Not for the first time, Perdie wondered if Rachel could possibly be getting enough to eat. Her huge blue eyes, outlined thickly with black liner, only made her cheeks look thinner. Heavy masses of dark hair that her father refused to let her cut hung down her back like a cape into which she might disappear.

"Mom!" Rachel sounded exasperated, as always. "What do you want?"

"I just … I'm going to have to go pick up Travis from his practice after dinner. Can you help me put the dinner dishes away later?"

Rachel rolled her eyes, a grim set to her mouth perfectly painted with dark-purple lipstick. "Sure. As if that will help."

Perdie ignored Rachel's comment, as she always ignored any reference to her husband's temperament. Not because she discounted her children's feelings, but because she simply had no response to give. She couldn't make it better, couldn't make sense of it. It simply was.

And Matt did love them, after all. He said so all the time. And clearly it was true — his whole life revolved around them. His every mood was subject to them. He'd be lost without them. He just had — weaknesses — of his own. He needed things to be a certain way, or he couldn't manage. And he'd done everything to build this life for them. The least they could do was keep his home, his refuge, safe and happy.

Hunching her backpack higher on her shoulder, Rachel tossed her hair back. "Is that all?"

"Oh, yeah. Sure. Do you have a lot of homework tonight?"

"Always. I'm in high school, Mom. Homework is the whole point, apparently."

"All right. I'll let you get started then."

Perdie stood for a moment, staring at her daughter's door as it closed behind her, her hands feeling awkward and over-large at her side. She didn't know what she was supposed to do. Were all teenagers this determined to avoid their parents at all costs? Hannah had been much the same. Minus the dramatic make-up and door-slamming, though. Hannah had been her ghost-child, drifting silently door to door through the house until she drifted out. Where no one could miss petite Rachel in a room, her taller, paler sister with her willowy, silent gait and dark eyes that warned away unwary gazers was usually remembered only in her absence.

Like now, thought Perdie with a sigh. Hannah was in her second year of college. There'd been no question of where she'd go, since Matt's professorship ensured tuition-free educations for his children. First-year students were required to live at home or in the dorms, and as soon as Hannah had completed her second semester, she'd found two roommates and moved out of the house before summer had hardly begun. Perdie had been surprised that Matt hadn't put up more of a fight, but then, Hannah hadn't really asked. She'd simply presented the move as a *fait accompli*, quietly and swiftly packed up, and disappeared. Now Perdie rarely saw her oldest and only heard from her when Perdie called her. Perdie didn't know if she was supposed to feel relieved that she'd raised such a capable and independent person or devastated that the thread she thought she'd tied to Hannah's heart on the day she was born had come so thoroughly unravelled.

But there was no time to be maudlin, Perdie scolded herself.

A fresh Waldorf salad was prepared and waiting in the

refrigerator, and a large baked-spaghetti pie was ready to go in the oven by the time Tad came in the front door. He was the real wild-card, Perdie knew. Rachel had seen enough, was old enough, that she could generally be counted on for what Perdie thought of as a "stressful evening." Tad was something different.

People always laughed about too many women in one house, but Perdie thought two men in one home was a thousand times harder. Tad had been such a self-possessed little baby, the brown eyes he'd gotten from his mother always weighing, always measuring. It hadn't helped, Perdie reflected sadly, that he looked more like her than like his father. Matt seemed to take that as an act of rebellion along with everything else.

Not that anyone would accuse Tad of being too self-possessed these days. Regret sat heavily in Perdie's stomach, sour and lingering. He'd been her strongest little soul, seemingly entirely himself from the first breath he drew, and now he was the most broken. She never knew from day to day which shard of himself he'd be carrying through the door, if its prism would cast light into their gloomy rooms or cut everyone it met.

It was just too hard, she told herself, for two men to be penned up in one house together. One day, when Tad was able to get out on his own, things would be different. Just a few more years. She could manage that, couldn't she? Couldn't he?

She yanked herself back from the precipice of that thought. Hope, she'd learned the hard way, was a fool's luxury. For ten years now, she hadn't allowed herself to imagine an end to this life, hadn't indulged in one moment's fantasy about escape. The only thing crueller than a prison was the promise that one day, the key would turn.

Not that she lived in a prison, Perdie hastened to reassure

herself. They had a beautiful home. A beautiful life. Every family had its own struggles. Just look at poor Julie. All those years devoted to her husband and children, and for what? So he could despise her for not being any more exciting than he'd allowed her to be? So he could think of her as the safety net he'd fall back into when his flings abandoned him? And now Julie was struggling to work full time and be a mom, and mostly failing at both. At least Matt would never cheat on Perdie. He adored her. He was just ... impatient. And she was sometimes too tired to do well. And sometimes the children were just too frustrating. She got frustrated, too. How could anyone blame Matt for losing his head from time to time? Everyone knew what it was like to raise teenagers.

And he'd forgiven her for that moment of weakness, ten years ago. Of disloyalty and selfishness. The fall-out from her unexecuted plan had been terrific, but she'd deserved it. What husband wouldn't be devastated to learn that his wife had been plotting behind his back to leave him, to steal his children? She'd been so relieved when he'd forgiven her in the end. Wrapped her bruised body gently in his arms and murmured his love, undying, unchanged by her infidelity, into her ears. Petted and praised her as she hadn't remotely deserved, feted and wooed her for weeks with dinners and dates out. There'd been no question of her leaving since then.

And wasn't that for the best? Just look what Julie was going through. At least Julie had friends and family to help her. The only way Perdie could ever have left Matt would have been to place thousands of miles between them, start over in a place with no help, no assurances of survival. As hard as it was to juggle all the chores and yard work and the kids' schedules now, Perdie couldn't imagine attempting it all with one or two full-time jobs on top of that.

But sometimes, in unwary moments like this, looking at her son, she wished for something different.

Then she didn't. She resolutely did not.

"Hi, honey," she said, barrelling into her son with the requisite hug she made sure none of her children could avoid. They were duty-bound by puberty to resist it, she knew, but she still believed that somewhere deep inside they wanted the hug anyway. "How was your day?"

"Fine," he muttered, same as always, with the same clumsy pat on her back. She was careful not to flinch, when his hand, over-sized for his still-bony wrist, grazed the belt-mark under her blouse. It was nearly healed now, anyway.

"I have to go pick up Travis from practice after dinner," she told him, knowing he would understand what she meant. "Do you want to go with me?"

"Not particularly."

"But you will?"

"How about I just stay in my room? I have a ton of algebra."

"It won't take more than 30 minutes, I promise. And we can stop by the coffee kiosk and get something to drink on the way home."

"Fine," Tad relented with what Perdie felt strongly was her least favourite word in the English language. She reached up and brushed his nearly military-short hair.

"Thank you."

She breathed a sigh of relief as Tad disappeared down the hall toward his room.

Too soon, as it turned out.

CHAPTER EIGHTEEN

"Think we have enough carbs on the table?" Matt asked, his brow arching.

Perdie smiled self-deprecatingly. "I know, I know. I wasn't thinking. At least we have salad to take the edge off."

She'd been focused on cooking his favourite foods, and she hadn't realised till too late that they didn't exactly form the most balanced menu. Rye bread and cinnamon butter, baked spaghetti pie (that's pasta and pie crust, so double carbs there), and the Waldorf salad.

"Lucky for me I get my exercise walking around campus all day," Matt said, piling his plate high as if he hadn't just stated his misgivings. "This looks delicious, Perdie. Rachel, you should eat more than that. You're going to waste away."

He smiled fondly at his daughter, who had maybe two bites worth of the spaghetti spread out beside a plateful of salad, as if to make it look more substantial. "I had a big lunch," she muttered, pushing the greens around with her fork. "I'm not that hungry."

Tad had no compunctions about the carbs. He was already

shovelling in pasta and cheese sauce, eyeing the pan as if planning for seconds. Perdie cut her food into precise tiny pieces, chewing each bite carefully as if to make it last. It was a trick she'd read in a magazine that was supposed to make you feel full sooner so you would eat less. She watched her weight like she watched everything else, forever anxious that any imbalance, any imperfection would jeopardise the fragile peace.

"Julie needs some extra help tonight," she began, keeping her eyes on her plate. "She has to work late, so I told her I would pick up Travis from practice and take him home for her. It shouldn't take more than half an hour. Tad can go with me."

Matt sighed, shaking his head. "I'm sympathetic, of course, but it just seems so selfish."

"What does?" Perdie asked, knowing that her participation in the conversation was required, even when it meant walking on perilous ground.

"This insistence of hers on independence. It would be one thing if she were actually capable of it, but she's not. Everyone else has to pitch in and help her so she can live the life she wants. She doesn't seem to think about how her choices impact others."

This was not a new point of view. Perdie had made the mistake of defending Julie once before, and she wouldn't do it again. As far as Matt was concerned, once Darren had come back, it was Julie's responsibility as a wife and as a Christian to forgive him and take him back. Julie was just being obstinate, Matt had argued. Obstinate and unloving. Terrible qualities in a woman.

"I don't mind," Perdie offered, the sinking feeling in her belly telling her there was no avoiding the conclusion of this night. "The chores are mostly done. Rachel will clean up the kitchen after we eat, and Tad will come with me. I'll be back before you know it."

Matt shook his head. "I wish that were true. This is what I mean — it's just selfish of Julie to expect you to rearrange your whole evening so she can abrogate her duties. I appreciate your generosity toward your friend, but it's too bad her happiness comes before mine. You know I prefer a quiet evening. But you've given your word. Tad, though — Tad can stay here with me. There's no need to disrupt his night as well. And I imagine he has homework."

Tad kept eating, but his movements slowed, and his eyes flicked up toward his mother.

Perdie knew better, but desperation urged her to push a little harder anyway.

"It's only half an hour. He'll be fine with me."

Matt set his fork down and turned his head toward her. Perdie raised her gaze, knowing that avoiding his eyes would only enrage him further. His voice, like always, was soft.

"I don't know why you insist on arguing with me. You act as if you don't want to leave me alone with my own son. Do you know what that feels like? When your own wife implies that you can't be trusted as a father?"

"I'm sorry," Perdie said hastily, knowing the words were too little, too late, but unable to stop them from spilling out.

"It's all right," Matt returned gently, reaching for the trembling hand she obediently extended. "You better go so you're not late. I'm sure Julie wants him home on time."

"Of course. You're right." Perdie jumped to her feet, clearing her half-eaten dinner and being careful to set her plate on the counter without clanging the dish. "I'll be right back."

The quick drive to and from the high school seemed to take forever. Travis politely chatted from the passenger seat.

As she dropped him at his house, Perdie wondered, not for the first time, how Julie had managed to raise such a pleasant, well-adjusted kid in the midst of all her family's drama. Travis and Rachel were the same age, and they'd been playmates when they were little, but those days were long gone. They didn't dislike each other or anything; they'd simply drifted apart, and now when they were thrown together on social occasions, they regarded each other with a sort of clinical curiosity, as if uncertain of the other's species.

Without thinking, Perdie went through the motions of her usual routine as she approached her house: shutting off the radio, slowing her speed to a crawl, pushing her seat back so that it would accommodate Matt's longer frame. He rarely drove her vehicle, but she'd learned it was best to be prepared.

She wasn't prepared, though. Not really.

On quiet feet, she moved from the garage into the kitchen. She supposed it was a strange reaction, but the angrier Matt was, the quieter she became. It was as if she imagined that she could curl up into herself, hedgehog style, and wait for the storm of fury and violence to simply blow over. She had no instinct for self-preservation, apparently, no reflexive answer of blow to blow. She'd never even considered the possibility of defending herself. Almost contrarily, her every movement would grow smaller and smaller, her voice softer and softer, till she was perfectly still and perfectly silent. Eventually, the noise and the pain would slow and cease — the noise, at least; pain had a tendency to linger — and then, after a few minutes, perhaps as long as an hour, the petting and the pampering would begin.

Matt would settle her into their big four-poster bed, propping up the pillows behind her and covering her with warm, fluffy blankets. He'd bring her a cup of tea and whatever book she was reading. He'd stroke her hair and beg her not to make him do that ever again. He might even cry, though he did that less and less these days. There was an order to their relationship, a ritual that had come to mean comfort to her in a weird and terrifying sort of way. She dreaded the blows, but she craved the affection, the worshipful kindness that eased away the achiness and promised unfailing devotion. She didn't want to do this, but she knew how. She could get through. She could endure, just one more time. She only had to endure one time at a time. Sufficient unto the day, she told herself silently. And maybe this would be the last time.

But when she stepped into the living room, she saw that Matt's fury was already spent. He sat slump-shouldered in his big recliner, his head resting on his wrist as a figure of despair. He didn't look up at the sound of her footfall, but his gravelly voice reached her across the room.

"You shouldn't have left me here alone. I told you I need my peace."

All Perdie's quiet left her, like the air leaving a root cellar when a tornado sweeps overhead. She barely recognised the howl that came from her as her own.

"No!"

Without a second thought, she left him there, fear suffusing her with a hot strength that propelled her down the hall, up the stairs, through the door to Tad's room. The kids weren't allowed locks on their doors, of course. She burst through, slamming the door shut behind her, and staring at her son with wide, wide eyes that felt as if they would never close again.

Tad was pressed into the corner of his bed, his bony, jean-clad knees pulled into his chest, his shoulders so tight against the wall Perdie wondered that he hadn't disappeared into the sheetrock. His algebra book lay open beside him, and his shaking fingers were scrawling across the notebook propped against his knees, working out equations as if his life depended on it. He'd flinched, hard, when she flew in the room, but he didn't raise his eyes, didn't look at her.

"Tad," she whispered, all her noise whooshing out of her.

"Why didn't you take me with you?" His voice was thick with tears. Boys, Perdie had learned, cried much harder and much longer than girls did. Even so, she hadn't seen Tad cry for at least two years now.

There was no good answer to that question. "I'm sorry," Perdie managed. "I'm so, so sorry."

She crossed the room, moved the algebra book. "Show me," she said. Matt was no fool. He never struck where a teacher or a neighbour might remark. Faces and forearms were off-limits.

"No." Tad did look at her then, and she blinked at the raw hate she saw flashing in his brown eyes. She wanted to believe that all that hatred was for Matt, but she knew that she had earned her share this night, too.

She didn't ask again. Her son had lost so much, she wasn't going to demand his dignity as well by forcing him to take off his shirt so his mother could count his wounds. She reached for him, though, her hesitant hand resting on his wiry arm. She felt the soft scruff of his man hair, the trembling of the child caught in the growing body.

"Rachel?" she asked softly.

Tad shook his head, a short, abrupt movement, understanding the question. "Why don't you ask her? I have homework."

She didn't want to go. She wanted to stay, to wrap her little boy up in her arms and promise him that this would never happen again, that she would keep him safe, that his father had been a good man once and would be a good man again. She wanted to stroke his hair and soothe his trembling and rock him to sleep in a world where fear would never threaten him. But she couldn't do any of that. So she backed away as he determinedly bent his attention back to his books and quietly closed his bedroom door behind her.

She dreaded facing her daughter almost more than she'd dreaded facing her son.

"Rachel?" she ventured, peeking around the corner of the door as she eased it open.

"Look who it is," Rachel returned bitterly. Unlike her brother, she made no pretence at caring about her school-work. She was sitting on the black beanbag on the floor, her make-up streaked with tears, her phone in her hand. Her fingers were flying over the tiny screen, and she shot her mother only the briefest, most scathing of glances.

"Need an update? Come to find out just what happened when you decided to do what you were told and leave your son here?"

"Rachel, I'm so sorry. I had no idea — I didn't think — he's never — it's always just me." Her words were a jumble of the lies and excuses she'd been telling herself for twenty years, and they tasted bitter as they left her mouth.

"Even you don't believe that," her daughter responded contemptuously. "If you really didn't think he'd ever go after Tad, then why do you always take him with you any time you leave the house? Because. You. Knew. Better. But this time, you left him anyway."

Perdie didn't have any more lies to offer. She went down on her knees beside her daughter, reaching for her arm as she had for her son's, "Tell me what happened. Please."

Rachel shrugged her away. "I'm pretty sure you can figure it out. He started in on him as soon as you left. I came up here, but then I heard a crash. I went downstairs, and he was all over him. I ran over and tried to stop him, but—" she swallowed hard, the tears welling back up and spilling over again, "he pushed me down."

Stunned, Perdie felt as if a kaleidoscope had broken, all the shattered, jagged pieces falling around her in a shower of colour and distorted shapes. Rachel was right — Perdie had been afraid for years that one day Matt would turn on Tad, but she'd never, ever, imagined that he would lay a hand on his daughters. They'd been sacrosanct, somehow, the precious princesses he adored. And if she was stunned, Rachel must have been beyond shocked. Hurt. Frightened.

"I'm going to kill him," Rachel gritted out, returning her attention to her phone. "I'm going to kill him."

"Oh, honey." Perdie tried again to reach out to her daughter, to stroke her hair, but Rachel moved away. "Don't say that. I'm so sorry. And I know your dad is sorry, too. I'll fix this. I promise. I'll fix this somehow."

Her daughter's eyes flicked up, a desert of hope, an oasis of hatred. Perdie backed quietly out of the room.

CHAPTER NINETEEN

Manage, manage, manage. Perdie had been living in this fogland so long, she no longer looked for light. Instead, she counted steps in the twilight, maintaining a slow and regular shuffle at all times to avoid banging into obstacles or tumbling over cliffs. So, while you are anticipating some vengeful fury, some reckless rage, a veritable Valkyrie of motherhood rushing down those stairs and destroying her husband, you couldn't be more wrong.

You see, while fear, anger, and pain might be triggers for you, they are nothing more than ambient reality to Perdie. Even this, the worst of all possibilities, that her children would one day become victims of their father's violence as well, was an event that she had anticipated, played out in her mind, a thousand times prior to this.

So, as Perdie walked down the stairs, she was counting the seconds of her inhales and exhales. One, two, three, four, five, six, seven, eight, nine, ten ... Ironically enough, it was the Lamaze technique she'd learned when pregnant with Hannah that had become her primary coping mechanism in this relationship. That, and the slow, regular, precise folding and unfolding of the hem of her blouse. She smoothed her features, preparing herself to face Matt as she rounded the steps.

But she wasn't prepared for what stood in his eyes, gleaming at her across the dimly lit living room.

Fear.

Raw, naked fear.

Only for a second. He blinked, and the fear vanished, replaced by the usual muddy mix of anger, resentment, and blame. But she'd seen it. She knew she had.

You aren't surprised, though, are you? You know what I know — that humans only do what they're allowed to do, and they are forever afraid of running up against the end of their possibilities. Matt hit Perdie for all sorts of reasons, but one of them was quite simple: she let him. He didn't hit the children because somewhere, at some point along the line, they'd made an unspoken, unbreathed pact that he couldn't. That Perdie wouldn't allow that. That's probably part of why you aren't all that fond of poor Perdie herself in this incarnation. For all that she imagines herself the victim, the truth is that she sets the rules, and he follows them. And her rules frankly suck, right?

I mean, on paper, you all get very huffy about the idea of trading money and security for pain and suffering. Sure, Perdie's rules meant that the children couldn't be physically touched by their father, but what about all the psychological trauma? What about listening to their father's blows landing on their mother's body, night after night? What about the atmosphere of fear and tension that permeated every breath, every bite of food in that house? It was a bad trade, you want to say.

Generally speaking, though, you don't care for the realities of the alternative, either. A woman's odds of being killed by an abusive partner increase astronomically when she makes the decision to

leave. And there are all the dynamics of being a single mother —
likely to require some sort of government assistance, absolutely
guaranteed to be largely absent from the children's daily lives. If
she's going to work and put food on the table and keep a roof over
their heads, she's not going to be the Super-PTA mom, too, showing
up with treats at parent—teacher conferences, cooking breakfast in
the morning, helping with homework in the afternoons, tucking
them into bed at night. She's a loss in your estimation, no matter
which way she turns — either her children are poorly supervised
runabouts lacking discipline and oversight, or she's the monster who
forces them to live in a home of violence and fear.

And unsurprisingly, Perdie thinks just like you do. That's why,
when she was staring around at the rubble of her children's lives —
and Tad's death — she'd imagined that she could manage all the
possibilities, all the probabilities, and make a better deal.

She'd thought she could take all the suffering in her own body
and spare her children. Kind of a god-like notion, don't you think?
But any bard will tell you those tales end in tragedy and not
triumph.

Regardless of how silly it all was, Perdie and Matt had had a
deal, though. And now he'd broken it. So, yes, he was scared. And
Perdie may be unremarkable in many ways, but she's not an idiot.
She seized her advantage.

"You hit the kids." Her voice was low, unshaken.

Normally, Matt's response to a cold condemnation like
that would have been swift and brutal. But he knew the game
had changed, and he knew she knew, too.

"I know." He summoned up a few tears from his regular
reserve. "I can't believe this has happened. I wish to God you
hadn't left him here with me."

This household had been so sick for so long that neither of
them questioned the preposterous reality of a father never

being alone with his own son. For the first time in a long time, though, Matt's victim-blaming excuse for an apology fell flat.

"You wanted me to." Perdie wasn't backing down — not yet. Her words hit the floor like stones. She resisted the urge to pick them up, put them somewhere out of sight.

"I know. This is totally my fault. I know better. He's too close to you. Immature. Disrespectful. I should have known that he would start misbehaving as soon as you left. This was my mistake. I'm so sorry. I promise I will make it right."

Anger, long stultified by self-loathing, stirred in Perdie's belly. She recognised the flavour of manipulation, and her lips pulled away from her teeth in disgust.

"He's not immature. He's fourteen. He has the emotional and intellectual ability of a normal fourteen-year-old boy. You are the adult. There's no excuse for what you've done. And Rachel—"

"You're right. I'm agreeing with you," Matt insisted in complete disingenuity, advancing on her and gathering her hands gently in his own. "That's what I'm saying. That this is my fault, and I'm sorry."

"I don't think sorry will fix this. They are both really hurt — and I don't just mean physically."

"Tell me what to do." Unexpectedly, Matt went down on his knees, pulled her against him, burying his head in her thighs. "Tell me what to do, and I'll do it."

And there it was. Even as a mother, Perdie lacked the instinct for a kill. This lion crouched at her feet, paws and jaws bloodied, tail down, tears in its eyes, and she could not bring herself to take a knife to its throat. Instead, she folded herself up apologetically and placed herself tenderly between his teeth.

"Therapy," she croaked out. "I think we need therapy."

She meant to say, "I think you need therapy," but it

sounded too harsh, too accusatory to her ears. So she softened her words, and he seized on the opening she left.

"You're right," he said humbly, keeping his head pressed against her so that she could not see the triumph shining in his eyes. "I've never wanted to consider it before, but you're right. Our family dynamics are all out of whack, and I think the stress just overwhelmed me."

Just in the nick of time, he stopped himself from launching into a litany of his wife's and his children's failings, some rarely needed sense of self-preservation intruding on his speech. Perdie's hands settled awkwardly on his head, patting him reluctantly.

"What else?" he said instead. "How can I make this up to you?"

"You need to apologise to Tad and Rachel," she said firmly, though she felt disloyal for making the suggestion. She wasn't sure what it was in her belly that told her that her children would not thank her for that. It was the right thing to do, though, wasn't it? Apologise when you'd done wrong? So why did she feel like she was hurting her children worse by suggesting it?

You probably know the answer to that question, too. It's one of the oldest tricks in an abuser's book: put on a show of abject humility to force the victim to either forgive you or else be in the wrong. Of course, the victim won't be able to do more than ape the words as their preacher has told them they ought — I forgive you — and that creeping, secret knowledge that they haven't forgiven you at all will eat at them, so that the next time you strike, they will truly believe they deserved it. Learned shame and guilt are far more powerful weapons than fists. The irony is that the actual guilty person feels none, only pretends it long enough to convince the innocent that they alone are the true ignition point of the violence. That their unmerciful heart deserves the battering. It's a beautiful cycle, almost inescapable.

The obvious truth is that it's not fair to even ask for forgiveness until you've demonstrated repentance; but preachers don't often say that, and abusers never do.

Perdie had been trapped in the cycle so long herself, she couldn't have ever identified what was wrong with it. But still, something in her heart twisted painfully at the idea of her children being forced to sit there, looking in their father's tearfully remorseful eyes, and tell him that it was all okay, while their bruises still coloured like starbursts.

But what else could she do? Those were the rules, weren't they?

"Of course," Matt said hastily, rising to his feet and pressing a fervent kiss to the top of her head. "I'll do that right now."

Perdie couldn't bring herself to go with him. She told herself that it was because it wasn't her place, that both the children and Matt deserved privacy to mend this relationship on their own. That her own emotional state would only be a distraction to the healing that needed to take place. The truth was, she couldn't stand in her children's doorways and see the look in their eyes when they realised that she, once again, had brought their father into their rooms.

There was no point in me tagging along. As I've already explained, I don't get any particular pleasure from cruelty or sorrow or even evil, strictly speaking. I'm just a choice arbiter. Sure, I'm always rooting for the side of pleasure and ease, partly because I think the whole system in unfairly rigged, and partly because who wouldn't choose the experience over contemplation of the experience?

There are two choices, as I see it. You can be a spiritual being in

*a carnal world, or a spiritual being in a spiritual world. And no.
There's no third or fourth option. There's no such thing as a carnal
being. Being necessitates the spiritual. That whole sentient thing is
more than stuff and dust and atoms. Anyway, I simply prefer
hedging my bets. Enjoying both sides of the bed. Why settle for just
the one sort of existence? Read all the existential poetry you want,
but invite pleasure under the sheets.*

*There weren't going to be any interesting choices laid out
upstairs tonight. Matt ceased being of any interest to me years ago. I
could bore you with the details of the exact moment when he passed
his tipping point, so to speak, and became thoroughly adhered to his
brutish nature, but I won't bother. And the kids? This wasn't going to
be one of their more scintillating moments, either. They would be
angry, resentful, hurt, and still — pathetically — wanting the very
people who'd put them into this position to get them out of it. So
they'd perform exactly as anticipated. The reluctant, audible
forgiveness, the self-loathing, the resentment, the bitterness, the
wistfulness unique to their years ... it was all too familiar to be
entertaining.*

Necessary, though, to get to the good bit.

CHAPTER TWENTY

Tuesday, Wednesday, and Thursday were good days for Perdie. Mindful of how near he'd stepped to that precipice from which there'd have been no recovery, Matt was more attentive than ever before.

Even I suffered a momentary trepidation, wondering if there'd been a corner I missed somewhere that he'd made his way around. There hadn't been, of course. Sometimes, though, even an old role takes on a new life.

Matt didn't limit his efforts to his wife. He wooed his children with the same tender intensity. A less adept man might have been bluff and cheery, but Matt was a master. He was penitent and sombre, slow of step and speech, deliberate in his choice of words and measure of eye contact. Never presumptuous, he hesitated and asked with his eyes before stepping in for his usual morning hugs.

In one sense, Rachel and Tad were as susceptible to good propaganda as Perdie was. It's simple human nature to feel relief when fear recedes. When the fist becomes the open palm, few victims seize the chance to run. Most take one step closer, tuck their bruised cheek against that palm, breathe in the sweet peace of pure affection. Whisper a quiet prayer of gratitude and tell themselves that this time, everything will be all right from now on.

The children did have one advantage, though. Where Perdie believed herself trapped — imagining that this sacrifice was the price she paid to provide for her children — Tad, Rachel, and Hannah lived in expectation of escape. After all, their whole purpose in life was to finish school and move away. Even the relief of a détente was not enough to rid their hearts of that steady beat: a-way, a-way, a-way.

Perdie didn't realise that, though. She was focused on moving forward and missed the warning signs. As, *let's admit it*, was her custom. Perdie had set her course ten years before, when she'd decided against her own escape. Ever since, her whole being had been bent on keeping her feet to the rocky path. Head down, knees knocking, she hadn't dared to look around, to gauge the terrain, to note the signs, for a very long time.

So Perdie researched family therapists, made phone calls, set appointments. She went to the Christian bookstore and came home with an armful of self-help marriage books and parenting worksheets, for which Matt expressed over-whelming gratitude. Come Friday night, when Rachel took advantage of her father's rare softening and asked to take the car out, Perdie hardly registered the act for what it was: open rebellion.

Matt hadn't been exaggerating about his expectations of unbroken tranquillity in the evenings. It had begun when the children were very young, and Perdie had found it simply impossible to meet Matt's standards when it came to meals and baths and regular bedtimes if she still had errands to run. Without a conscious effort, she'd taken to running errands and completing projects during Matt's working hours and holding the evenings sacrosanct. The rare exceptions would be if they had company over for dinner. On those occasions, she was spared any outbursts, as Matt was entirely focused on presenting himself the perfect husband and father to their guests, and his good humour usually lasted even after they left. It was as if he were recounting a fairy tale, and for a little while, he convinced himself of its truth.

As the children got older, it became harder, of course. Parent—teacher conferences were possibly the worst. Perdie had often wondered if the teachers ever suspected how the gracious, mild-mannered man with the easy smile would change when he got his family home and ate his late dinner. She'd tried, briefly, with Hannah, to be a sports mom, but swiftly she'd realised that was not an option for them. It was too stressful — for everyone, she'd insisted. Hannah hadn't made it one season of softball. Sports, band, theatre — none of these were options for the Blevins kids.

Adults have a gift when it comes to convincing themselves of things. Children are more natively resistant to falsehood — one reason why, even with all the practice they get, they remain terrible liars — but it grows on them over time. Children read books for the opposite reason as adults do: they're hunting for hidden truths, while adults are searching for palatable lies. Perdie liked to tell herself that all of her children were too individualistic, too independent, to need participation in group activities to feel content. Hannah was an artist, after all. Rachel's passion was fashion, and Tad — well, Tad was still figuring life out, wasn't he? He seemed equally enchanted by every study he undertook — photography, graphic novels, mycology. She could take Tad anywhere — an art gallery, an aerospace museum, a library, an aquarium — and he would be enthralled.

Where most people skim over life, restively seeking predetermined triggers they've identified as pleasurable, Tad soaked life in. He stood where he was, saw what he looked at, felt what he touched, heard when he listened. He'd have made an excellent sommelier. I can just see him: eyes closed, breathing in every delicate scent, luxuriating in the smooth wash of flavour over his tongue, tasting every unique and distinctive note where ordinary people merely tasted wine. I wouldn't be surprised if Tad saw the colours the rest of you simply don't discern; in fact, I'd be surprised if he didn't. I imagine he could hear the stars singing. You could too, for that matter, but odds are you don't listen.

Tad listened.

I say all this to explain what no doubt seems highly unlikely to you — that two angry teenagers would simply come home after school every day and go to their rooms. But that's what they'd been doing all their lives, and they were well aware of the consequences if they didn't. Even now, when they were at least as angry at Perdie as they were at their dad, neither of them would bear up well under the guilt of coming home to the sounds of their father's fists and feet slamming into their mother's body.

But on Friday evening, Matt merely smiled placidly when Rachel asked for the keys.

"It's probably about time you had some practice with that licence of yours. We can't very well expect you to be a good driver if you never get behind the wheel. Where are you going?"

"Just to the park. I'm taking Tad with me."

"That sounds good. Don't stay out too late. It's getting dark early now, and some bad characters hang out in the park."

Rachel managed to spin around before rolling her eyes.

Bad characters? Worse than you, Dad? she wanted to ask, but she wanted the car more. Her father might be playing remorseful now, but she'd watched this cycle play out for her mother enough times that she understood she might have another day or two of grace at best, and she could abridge that herself with the wrong word.

"Come on, Tad," she yelled up the stairs. Instantly, Tad appeared, clearly waiting out of sight for her cue, his backpack clutched in his arms.

"Hey, son," Matt said, standing by the front door so that Tad would have to pass him to leave the house. Perdie watched the little scene play out from the kitchen doorway, her arms crossed over her breasts and her eyes cynical. She recognised this dynamic too well. Clearly Matt was already tiring of his meek position in relation to this son, this man whose challenge was inherent in his hormones. Matt might make it longer where his wife and daughter were concerned, but with Tad, he wanted — no, needed — to reassert himself.

The man's power over his family was as much, if not more, in the tiny, relentless, deliberate impositions of his will over theirs as it was in the fantastic explosions of rage. Matt knew that his son had done his best to avoid him since the "incident," knew that he'd hidden in his room except for the requisite dinner table appearance. It was unacceptable that Tad wouldn't make himself available for his father's wooing and penance. Refusing to play along with Matt's apology play was an act of rebellion that would not be countenanced.

So Matt stood by the door with a smarmy smile on his face, waiting for his son to hunch past him to his sister and the outdoors. As Tad stepped into the pale twilight gleaming beneath the open lintel, his father reached out and patted him vigorously on the shoulder. Tad flinched visibly and pushed through, only stopping once he reached his older sister's side, looking back at his father with a flinty, grim expression.

Perdie tracked the flash of anger that transformed her husband's face into a demon's, just for an instant, then vanished behind his eyes as if it had never been.

I'm using that term — demon — figuratively, of course. Let's not even get started on that rabbit hole. Suffice it to say that humans don't require a moment's assistance to achieve the lowest levels of evil, certainly not from my people. The only demons walking this earth today are you.

"Have fun," gritted Matt easily. Perdie understood that this transparency, this seeming near-loss of temper, was nothing of the sort. Matt had long ago perfected his discipline. If anyone saw his rage, it was only because he wanted them to. Theirs was a complicated dance, with precise steps and deliberate patterns, and each of them knew their places when the music began. She didn't begrudge her children for walking off the dance floor, if only for a few brief hours. Whatever the cost, it was a joy to watch them step just out of his reach.

CHAPTER TWENTY-ONE

Bat out of hell. Do you ever really think about that imagery? Tiny little bright-eyed furry creature, expending every ounce of energy and just managing to carry its leathery wings out of reach of the flames, escaping into the cool, fresh rush of air unseared by sulphur and fire? The desperation and terror, the relief and exhilaration, of that moment? Well, you should. People use that imagery as if it were funny, but it's poignant, awful, and fearsomely rare.

That was how Rachel was feeling that evening, and, yes — her driving reflected that.

Tad wisely kept his observations on that score to himself, still clutching his backpack against his chest, over his seatbelt, staring blindly out the windshield for several minutes before speaking.

"Where are we going?" he finally asked.

"Nowhere. Anywhere. Where do you want to go?"

"You told Dad we were going to the park."

"So? It's not like he's going to come looking for us," Rachel bit off, though that was anything but certain. "Besides, we're not five. We can go where we want."

"Ice cream?" Tad offered.

Rachel snorted, casting her brother a fondly contemptuous look. "I take it back. Maybe you are five. But sure. We can do that."

A fine, November drizzle was falling, coating the roads with moisture as the temperatures dropped. More than once, the wheels spun as Rachel whipped in and out of the cars, with no more intent than the simple pleasure of the speed and the fear. Part of her wished wildly, blindly for nothing but speed, nothing but acceleration and its sudden, complete annihilation, free of any thought or anxiety or trepidation, a darkness where she couldn't count seconds, couldn't count steps, couldn't count bites and calories.

She cast a glance at her little brother, at the fine, tight lines of his silhouette, and reluctantly pulled herself back from the precipice. She'd been looking out for him for too long to abandon that role now, no matter how tempting the abdication. He needed her. And of all of them, she thought, he was the one who might make it. Her mother didn't realise it, but Hannah was already well and truly broken in pieces.

Hannah was three years older than Rachel, the first-born daughter to be placed on her father's pedestal where the view was impossible to escape. With all the responsibility and guilt incumbent on the eldest, she had taken the weight of every blow that struck her mother into her own small body, her permanent exclusion from her father's rage a terrible gift that perhaps cost more than the brutal tariff might have done. Rachel, following behind and too young to fully understand, had nonetheless watched helplessly as her sister tore off pieces of her soul, shredded them into tiny pieces, and set them adrift on the wind. Rachel watched until she thought, surely, there was nothing left of Hannah. The quiet creature who drifted through the family hallways and one day drifted out the front door was empty, bare, having taken all the vulnerable fragments of her heart and given them to the ether for safekeeping. Rachel didn't know if Hannah would ever be able to find them again, if she would ever be able to put herself back together.

As for Rachel herself — she didn't have much hope for her own survival. She wasn't sure she wanted hope. What she wanted was an excess of feeling. She was so sick of control, of caution, of measure, measure, measure. She wasn't picky about what the emotion was: anger, fear, jealousy, revenge, spite, joy, exhilaration. More than anything, she wanted a moment to simply be, overflowing, overwhelmed, flamboyant, out-of-control, thoroughly given over to anything, anything at all. She suspected when the time finally came, it would be the end of her, but it would be worth it. Just to live, for a second, would be worth any death.

Precisely the longings I treasure most. Rachel had become a masterpiece of frustrated ache and want. Forced into silence when she would sing, she was a lovely porcelain nightingale, ready to shatter into symphony when I finally broke her.

The wheels skidded again as Rachel pulled into the strip mall parking lot that housed the ice cream shop. Tad silently clutched the car door, and Rachel laughed as she wrenched the steering wheel too hard and the car nearly spun out before straightening out.

Not tonight, though, she told herself, savouring the little rush of adrenaline. Tonight she was taking Tad for ice cream. She wondered how Tad would remember his sisters when he was the only one left.

Tad clambered out of the car with obvious relief on his face, but he grinned when he met his sister's eyes.

"You know you can't drive at all, don't you?"

"Nonsense," Rachel said, tossing her hair. "I'm a very consciously bad driver. I drive exactly as I intend to."

"Oh, geez, isn't that reassuring." Tad was still grinning, though, clearly enjoying their small freedom as much as she did.

Unsurprisingly, on a cold grey winter night, the ice cream shop was deserted but for the shovel-faced woman behind the counter. She dished up a double-fudge sundae for Tad with cherries and nuts both, and a small cup of fat-free frozen yogurt for Rachel.

"Come on," Rachel said, grabbing a fistful of paper napkins as she jerked her head toward the door.

If she made it to adulthood, Rachel would have recognised all the little habits she'd acquired to sidestep her father's excuses for anger, all the accommodations that had become second nature. But we don't have that long with this Rachel here.

"Where now?"

"Somewhere we can really enjoy this ice cream."

Tad shrugged, already a third of the way through his dessert. He didn't care where they went. This little island of time alone with his sister, out of that house, was its own reward. And ice cream was literally the cherry on top.

Still, he was surprised when his sister pulled the car on to the gravel paths that wound through the cemetery. Night had fallen in earnest now, and the car's headlights flashed macabrely on the flat, gleaming surfaces of ice-slicked tomb-stones. It was as if some light from the graves themselves shone out and greeted them, one by one.

"Well, I didn't realise this was the ideal place to eat ice

cream," Tad offered humorously. "Too bad I already finished mine."

Sure enough, his spoon rattled forlornly in the empty plastic boat bereft of all but the scarcest vestiges of ice cream and chocolate. Rachel shook her head exasperatedly and shoved her own cup at him.

"Here, you can have mine," she told him. "I'm full anyway."

"Full? You had, like, three bites. Besides, that stuff is nasty. It tastes like a wet tissue. I'm going have to insist you finish that yourself."

Rachel shrugged, but her eyes did slide longingly to the frozen yogurt melting over the plastic spoon.

"Seriously. There's no point wasting it. Besides, we don't have anywhere to throw it away if you don't eat it," Tad urged her.

Rachel cut the engine, and the headlights fell into darkness. A full moon gleamed hazily from behind the drifting clouds. Slowly, their eyes adjusted to the grey, and they watched the sleet become snowflakes quietly blanket the sentinel stones.

"Mom's never going to fix this, you know," Rachel said finally. She didn't know why she was nearly whispering, as if reluctant to shatter the delicate peace wrought by snow and darkness.

"I know," Tad whispered back, matter-of-factly. "She can't."

"You know I'm not going to leave him alone with you, don't you?"

"You have to leave eventually. You graduate next year. And there's no reason for you to be stuck just because I am. You should go when you can. Hannah left."

Rachel thought about her ghost of a sister again. She'd felt the same betrayal she heard in Tad's voice now when Hannah had gone to college; but she didn't feel that way anymore. The truth was that Hannah had left long before she'd gone away, and it wasn't Hannah's fault. Her tether had been too frayed, too battered. She couldn't hold her place, not for herself, not for her siblings.

"Maybe I have to go, but I don't have to leave you with him."

Tad's gaze sharpened, his dark eyes seeking hers in the gloom of the car interior, unlit by stones or snowlight.

"What are you thinking, Rach? You know it will only get worse if we tell."

This was not a new conversation. As small children, the realities of their existence had been too ingrained to ever consider looking for help outside their own four walls. Then they'd understood that every aspect of their survival came only from within, and that to violate the sacred pact of family by bringing outsiders into their private agonies would have been more than unforgivable — it would have been nonsensical. As they'd gotten older, the notion had grown more attractive, but by then they understood the mundanities of the process that rendered it worse than useless.

Anyone they told would be obligated to investigate. Even if their mom chose to press charges — which seemed highly unlikely, given that she'd never even openly acknowledged what was happening — there'd only be an arrest, a bail hearing, and then he'd be home again. No protection order could alter that. And the consequences of their rebellion would be far worse than anything they'd endured before, there was no question about that. The process offered them no hope at all. There was always the looming possibility that the state might actually take them out of their home, and while they could accept being torn from their mother, they could not accept being torn from each other.

"I know. I'm not going to tell. I just want you to know you

don't have to worry. She might not be strong enough to do anything, but I am."

Tad unbuckled his seatbelt, shifted his body so he was facing his sister.

"Don't do anything stupid, Rachel. You're almost out of here. I won't be far behind. And I'm not going to go to Ohio State. I'm getting as far from here as I can."

"But the tuition at Dad's college is basically free."

"I won't need it. I'm getting a scholarship. Why do you think I'm actually doing my homework? You know, you could do the same thing."

Rachel laughed bitterly. "I think it's a little late for me on that score. Besides, I'm not half as smart as you are. You even make chemistry look easy."

"It is easy. Remember that block-shape table from when we were little? That's all it is. Find the shape, drop it in. Everything matches up perfectly."

"Maybe in your head, nerd. The rest of us don't have block-shape tables for brains."

Tad shrugged. "I'm just saying, don't do anything crazy. We'll get out. Soon. And then we don't ever have to come back."

Rachel's blue eyes darkened with sympathy. "You have to know things have changed, Tad."

"What do you mean?"

"Now that he's—" she stumbled over the next words, hesitant to say it out loud and grant it form, "hit you, he won't stop. He's been waiting years, and now he's gotten away with it. He'll be after you like he's after Mom."

"Except I can fight back," Tad said fiercely, still in a whisper.

"Will that really make it better?" Rachel asked incredulously.

"Yes," came the determined, unconvincing reply.

"Okay," Rachel relented wearily. "Okay. Maybe that will make it better. But it still isn't right."

"Lots of things aren't right," Tad insisted stubbornly. "Just — give it some time, Rach."

Rachel's gaze drifted back out the windshield, snagged on flake after flake as it tumbled slowly past. She put her hand on her brother's bony knee.

"All right," she promised quietly. "I won't do anything stupid."

CHAPTER TWENTY-TWO

Tad buckled his seatbelt, absently licking his empty spoon and staring out the passenger window into the dark. Snowflakes grabbed hands and clasped each other tight, falling faster and in thicker clumps. The sheen of moisture that had slicked the streets on their way to the cemetery had hardened into an icy pavement, and the car spun gently as Rachel backed her way out of the narrow path and headed for the entrance.

You can probably tell that Rachel and I have had some pretty intense late-night conversations, can't you? It's a sure bet that someone has been talking to me when they've already run through all the arguments before they ever breathe a word of their conflict aloud. In fact, of all the silly caricatures and outright monstrosities attached to me, that's the only one I can think of that's truly accurate: devil's advocate.

Now, in your culture, that's still an epithet of sorts, but it's a reasonable one. Devil's advocate is precisely my favourite game to play. Let's explore every possibility, every option, every turn in the road. Don't imagine there are ever only two choices. There may be only one choice They want you to make, but I'm endlessly flexible. I can find a road to pure physical delight through any impasse.

Are you caught up in the same cycle of arguments as Rachel is? Do you see a way out? Don't focus on principles, those will muddy any map. Eyes on the destination only.

I'm not trying to produce any more of what you would consider evil in the world. What I want is a Rachel thoroughly given over only to what this temporal world can offer. The pleasures and delights and comforts of the flesh. Though, you humans do possess a rather impactful obstacle to that level of dedication: your soul.

I have no use for souls. Frankly, they are a lot of baggage I'd rather divest myself of. However, as long as you allow those pesky things to define you, as long as you hunger after what the soul hungers after, as long as you yearn after the world beyond, I can't hold you to me with any certainty. At any moment, you could decide to cast my world aside and go streaking after the ephemeral.

You might remember earlier I alluded to the fact that it's not as either-or a proposition as I'd like it to be. Ironically, as long as you draw a physical breath, there's hope for your spiritual life. I've literally had people bury their soul under a pile of bodies, and then come back years later, dig through the rotting flesh, hold in their hands every ounce of carnage and grief that they caused, and retrieve that soul in the end. I don't understand the impulse, myself. It's bad enough that they committed the atrocities in the first place, when embracing my path requires far less in the way of trespass; but to go back and put themselves through bearing witness to it all over again just to gain entrance to a world that doesn't comprehend a whole hemisphere of their nature? Baffling.

Anyway, what I'm trying to say is that I take no delight in the atrocities themselves. Truly, they're repugnant. Once you start on that path, I lose all interest. You don't need my interference at that point to desecrate and destroy your own spiritual nature. You take care of that perfectly well on your own. You're not just repugnant —

you're downright boring and painfully predictable. I keep myself entertained by provoking to contemplation those of you who imagine yourselves impenetrable to my attacks.

I have no part in the fearsome acts you commit. There's no pleasure, no delight, to be found there. That is entirely you, an impulse I can't begin to understand. Once you start mixing that particular drink, I get as far away from you as I possibly can. Bile and cruelty aren't flavours that appeal to me. That mixology is only in your handbook.

Whenever evil enters the dialogue, thoughts frequently turn to the Holocaust. But that's a deflection. A way of putting evil so far outside you, making it so big, so overwhelming, that it can't possibly bear any relation to you — when, actually, evil is at your own elbow.

Let me give you an everyday instance, a common enough example whose twin you could find in a news column any day of the week, in any town. A little parable about how recklessly you discard what is beautiful.

Consider babies with me for a moment. They're precious, delightful little bundles of carnality. All they seek is everything I can offer them. They love soft blankets, warm arms, good food, clean skin, funny surprises. They have soft little delicate heads that wobble, tiny fingers that clutch at anything in reach, and a gift for taking pleasure that adults and even children have long forgotten. If you doubt how much they're mine, just watch one the first time she finds her toes. She's happy for ages just playing with toes. That's the sort of living in the moment that I thoroughly support.

But what do you do with that? Just the other day two of you left a baby to die in a baby swing over a period of two weeks. Can you imagine? That baby must have cried for days. I don't know how it all transpired myself; I'd left that place weeks before. And the parents hardly cared — in a fog of heroin and meth, they just wanted someone to dispose of the mess.

What possible interest could I have in a scenario like that?

Where's the choice? Where's the pleasure? Where's the conflict? Those people gave themselves over long ago, not even to pleasure, but to the dulling of all real sensation. Fools. This place is a wonderland. Addicts like that throw away heaven and don't even taste the earth. God might still try to win them over, but I wouldn't waste my breath.

I'm insulted, in point of fact, by the acts that you attach to my name. Do you really think you require any interference on my part to become monsters? You are monsters on the very face of the thing. A half-beast, as mythological as any griffin or centaur. Forever at war with one side or the other of your own selves. Not with me.

All I require is your isolation. Once I isolate you from those gifts of the Spirit (Their spirit, your spirit, there's not actually a difference) then I win. Without fealty, kindness, companionship, patience, grace, you'll chase down any meaty pleasure I offer to make up for the loss. And you're so easily defeated. I mean, angels have been known to devote themselves to winning Their affection and approval for what you'd count millennia before they give up. Not that I know anyone like that. But you are riddled with depression, anxiety, stress — all words for hunger, hunger that I can't fill, but I can surely provoke and tantalise. Something to tide you over, something to make you think you're happy, better off. You give up so swiftly. One rejection, one grief, is more than enough to send most of you spinning into my arms. Some of you hold out much longer, I grant you, but when offered the choice between one more loss and a sure delight, you choose the delight almost every time.

I'm not about pain and apathy, lethargy and numbness. Such can hardly tempt anyone. Even those who imagine they crave emptiness are really looking for escape, and escape from the existential agony of life suspended between heaven and earth is precisely what I offer. I'm about the smell of jasmine on a warm spring wind, the stroke of a tongue on a trembling thigh, the burst of a sun-warmed strawberry, the endlessly wonderful shapes of the snowflakes as they catch on your eyelashes. I'm about the strangely precise divisions that languages build in the heart, the tracks of the stars in the skies. I'm about music resonating in your bones, canyon walls climbing to the sky, the rush of a free, furious river over the boulders. And to my sorrow, to my sorrow, I'm about light, the way it strikes the eyes, illuminates glory, warms everything it touches.

Like you, I can't help but love the light. Love the way it changes and beautifies everything it touches. The light of the sun, the light of God, the light in you. But the price I pay for my choice is that I must always watch that light depart to a place I cannot follow. In all its colours, all its strength, I see it, feel it, on levels you can't even fathom; but still I can only watch it leave.

I hate my truth. I want to keep the light here, where it will play across all the landscapes I love. But the darker you are, the more light you steal from my world. I was angry when that baby's light left my plane, and those two black holes falsely named parents remained. As I was angry when Matt battered his wife like a coward instead of meeting her passion and fury with a beautiful, brilliant rage of his own that could have illuminated them both instead of choking them out in darkness. Or when he resented the mysterious ways his children's eyes lit up worlds he couldn't see instead of requesting entry to those strange places and learning new delights.

So, I don't want you to misunderstand the choices that Rachel and I discussed. I wasn't trying to convince her to commit any appalling act. I was only trying to isolate her. I wanted her to choose the course that would leave her most alone, so I could console her with all the simple pleasures she might otherwise resist in the name of family or friendship or love. I don't want you to be evil; I just want you to be alone. Whatever it takes to achieve that works for me. And remember: Rachel is only a secondary target for me in this story. I have plenty of time to reach her.

Tad clung to the armrest of his car door as his sister navigated the city streets back to their house. Caught up in the plot unravelling in her head, Rachel was more cautious than usual, and her road-worthy inexperience aside, managed to deliver them both safely back at home without wrapping the car around a pole or sending it careening into a ditch.

You might think I knew that already, but prescience isn't one of my gifts. Thankfully. How boring would that be? But it does mean that God and chance can interfere with my plans at any moment and curtail my efforts rather abruptly. I was pleased and relieved when the car pulled into the drive, and it appeared I'd get to play this all the way out.

Matt helped, as he always did.

Completely self-driven characters like him make excellent foils for my scenes.

CHAPTER TWENTY-THREE

Perdie had plainly done what she could. Post-smack honeymoon or not, Matt's tolerance for upset in his evenings was notoriously slight, and likely none of them truly expected to end the night unscathed.

When Rachel and Tad came in the garage door, the floors were sparkling and flickering candles in every room exuded deceptively calming fragrances. The kitchen had been cleaned up, the dishes put away, and the sharp scent of popcorn, Matt's favourite TV-watching snack, hung in the air.

Tad headed straight upstairs. He knew that he, more than anyone, was the catalyst for his father's anger. As dearly as Matt had wanted a son to carry on his name, his legacy, he resented another man in his domain, particularly one whose nature was so different from his own. All the things Tad couldn't control about himself — his height, his burgeoning testosterone, his growing strength — were silent affronts to Matt's own manhood. And the things he could control — those measuring glances, the stubborn self, the innate chivalry — those were even worse. The less Tad and his father interacted, the better for everyone. Even Matt knew it, but his son was a scab he couldn't resist picking.

Rachel tossed their ice-cream trash in the kitchen and stuck her head into the living room where Matt and Perdie watched television, the bowl of popcorn perched between them. "We're home," she declared shortly.

"Don't run off," her father protested, in that too-nice voice she'd come to loathe. "Come sit down with me and your mom."

Reluctantly, Rachel stepped into the living room and sat down in the chair. Her parents were on the love seat, watching something on the tv. At least, part of her was reluctant. Another part — the part that got bigger and stronger every time she heard her dad's fist collide with someone's body, the part that had been near-ravenous with growth since last Monday night — that part released a happy growl and settled more comfortably into her skin, ready for another feast.

"Did you guys have fun?" Perdie asked.

"Yeah. We got ice cream."

"Where's your brother?" Matt asked. "Avoiding his family, I take it."

"Naw," Rachel answered, quelling the quick flush of anger that prompted her to say, *of course he is*. Instead, she countered with the one excuse that always held true for her little brother: "He has homework."

"Maybe he should have thought about that before going out. Call me suspicious, but I don't see why your brother always seems to have three times as much homework as you or your sister did."

Rachel laughed outright at that, ignoring her father's narrowed eyes spearing toward her. "That's easy to explain. Hannah and I are too smart for that. You do realise that dumb kid is taking two sciences and a math this semester? I've got

Family Living and Business Accounting. He completely sets himself up for homework."

Matt struggled to find something derogatory to say about that, but he found himself entirely in a corner. So he changed tactics. "I thought you two were going to the park."

"We did. Park and ice cream." A cemetery is a sort of park, Rachel told herself. Headstones holding the place of slides from this world into the next, the same trees and hills, walking trails.

"You don't look like you've been out in the snow."

Beside her husband, Perdie shifted uneasily. She could feel his restless anger, hunting for a target.

"We weren't, not really. We mostly just sat in the car and watched the snow fall. It was colder than we expected."

"I'm surprised you'd have that much to talk about with a fourteen-year-old boy. Unless you just wanted out of the house so you could complain about your parents."

"Oh, yeah, it's all about you, all the time, Dad."

Matt only raised an eyebrow at her. "Maybe I should call Tad down here and ask him."

"Maybe you should do something with your evening besides make your kids miserable. I'm going to my room. Fight with yourself if you want."

"Young lady." His voice snapped against her back as she crossed the room to leave. She hesitated. "You can show respect, or you can be taught respect."

Rachel sensed her mother moving against her husband, patting his arm ineffectively in an effort to draw his attention away from her child and back to herself.

Rachel knew better, but she couldn't resist. "Respect has to be earned." She tossed her hair and forced herself to walk, not run, to the stairs, up into her room, slamming the door behind her with a satisfactory thud.

Her heart thudding out of her chest, breath rattling in and out, she waited in horrified anticipation, straining for footsteps over the roaring of her veins. She grabbed her desk chair as if she meant to shove it under her doorknob and froze, terrified by her own rebellion. Her father didn't allow locks on the doors for a reason. He believed it was his right to walk unimpeded into their rooms whenever he wanted. If he tried to open her door and found it blocked, he'd no doubt still make it through, but he'd be a thousand times angrier by the time the chair splintered and gave way. Still, every cell in her body cried out to stop him, slow him, toss any obstacle she could find into his path.

But the footsteps she was anticipating didn't sound on the stairs. She waited, knuckles white on the arms of the chair, forcing her breath to slow and quiet, but the footsteps didn't come.

Finally, she settled into something like a relaxed state, sliding down on to the floor with her back to the door and her phone in her lap. She was beginning to hear it now — raised voices from downstairs, the usual call-and-response. She clapped her headphones on and cranked up the volume, refusing to listen to it again.

Rachel thought she had a plan. She hadn't been exaggerating when she'd promised her brother that she wasn't going to leave him alone with their father. Telling anyone — a teacher, the police, a counsellor — would only increase the odds of their father laying hands on them. The wheels of justice are slow and precise. The time and space Matt would be afforded to prove his innocence was the same time and space he would use to prove his authority on the bodies of his family. Rachel could have run away, but she couldn't very well bring Tad with her.

She had no plan for survival, and little opportunity to

create one. She wasn't allowed an after-school job, and the allowance her parents gave her was a pittance, good for a treat now and then, but not enough to save for an escape. Ohio in winter was not kind to those on the streets, even where soup kitchens and community closets offered some resources. Hannah's tiny apartment already had three other people in it, and even if she tried to help, all her father had to do was withdraw his support for her tuition and board, and she'd be in the same state with the rest of them. She didn't even have a car.

So, running away wouldn't work unless Rachel was willing to abandon Tad and get as far away as fast as she could. But she couldn't leave her little brother behind.

As far as Rachel could see

— and I have to admit, I'm pretty proud of my ability to dictate what choices people imagine are available to them —

only one option remained.

She'd have to kill her father.

She'd watched enough documentaries and ID Investigates specials to be certain she could get away with it. Self-defence or battered-child syndrome, either one would do for a legal defence. She had no doubt that her mom would back her up. Perdie might be useless in most ways, but at least it wasn't for want of affection. Rachel didn't understand why her mother tolerated Matt's abuse like she did, but she did know that Perdie would come out on her children's side in the end. Knowing that didn't make Rachel any less angry at her mother for putting her in this position in the first place, though. All the options Rachel didn't have, Perdie still did, and she could have escaped with her children a hundred times over through the years. Not to mention she could have picked up a gun and finished the man off herself. Still, being angry at her mom didn't make Rachel any less assured of her loyalty when the time came.

The problem was that even a young girl who has been surrounded by violence and fear her entire life can't easily contemplate murder, much less actually carry it out. Killing someone in in theory is substantially less messy, not to mention less physically demanding, than doing it in real life.

For Rachel it was particularly difficult, because her father had pampered and spoiled her most of her life. She knew her father was a brute, knew he took out any rage and frustration and exasperation at his children on his wife, but she rarely had to even witness it and, until this week, had certainly never felt it on her own body. As much as she hated her father for being an abuser, she hated her mother for being a victim.

But that didn't mean she didn't also love them both. And not for the trite excuse that they'd brought her into this world and kept a roof over her head. She loved them for the Saturday afternoon picnics, the school plays, the Disney World vacations, the Sunday morning fights over who got to read the funny pages first and the Friday night fights over whether they were getting popcorn or Junior Mints at the movies. It didn't matter that all these memories were highly staged affairs for which her mother paid later; they were the fiction she'd read and believed her whole life. They mattered. And she did love her parents.

But Rachel had thought and thought and thought, and she couldn't find another way out. Now that her father had struck Tad and pushed her, she knew in her bones he wouldn't stop. This would become their new reality. Her mother had never rebelled before, and Rachel didn't believe she would now. She might try to defend them, but she'd demonstrated time and again that she was no match for her husband, so what differ-ence would that make? He'd only be that much angrier by the time he got past his wife to his children. But if Rachel killed him, if she stopped him, it would finally be over. No more fear. No more fights.

Intellectual acceptance and emotional readiness were two different things, though. Somehow, she'd have to reach a fever pitch of rage, a blind, overwhelming flood of fury that would carry her through the act. She couldn't afford a moment's hesitation, a moment's mercy. She couldn't risk looking into his eyes and seeing her daddy instead of the monster that lived under his skin. She needed to wake her own monster, feed her, provoke her, and let her go. Let her carry her past the moment and into the freedom that waited beyond.

The practicalities were a whole other issue, as well. Her father didn't own a gun. Maybe she could find one from one of the kids at school, but then she'd be subject to the whole issue of premeditation. Rachel was no fool; she knew that her chances of getting away with murder would go down astronomically if the police even suspected she acted with an ounce of deliberation rather than in the heat of the moment. And she couldn't think of one good reason for having a gun. No one would buy that she'd suddenly developed an interest in deer hunting.

She wasn't strong enough to strangle him, and she didn't think she could stare into his face as she stole his air, anyway. That left a knife as the only good option. She could hit him in the head with a blunt object, but short of actually smashing his skull in, that hardly guaranteed death.

And a knife still wasn't a fantastic option. She'd have to act fast, before he suspected what was happening, or he'd take it away from her. Attacking in his sleep would be safest, but Rachel didn't think she could get angry enough and scared enough to go after him while he slept. And it would also blow her story that she acted in self-defence. Maybe if she came up behind him while he was going after her mom or her brother. Even then, she knew she'd have to find the strength to strike again and again. To feel the blade slipping in her hand as the blood seeped and still not stop.

She needed to be ready, she told herself fiercely, desperately. She'd already made the decision. There was no turning back from here. It was only a matter of time. When the time came, she'd be the one to save them all. She just had to be ready.

I confess I was distracted by Rachel's perfect, lovely pride in this moment. I've developed some contempt of the familiar when it comes to selfishness. I appreciate that you're choosing satiation over sacrifice, but it's too common, too easy to bring me any delight. Illusions like Rachel's, though — that wonderful saviour complex capable of justifying the most outrageous of acts — those are my macaroons, my port wine, my sweetest indulgences. A trait she must have inherited from her mother.

The music blared on in Rachel's ears as she scrolled blindly through her social media accounts, clicking and swiping by rote. She barely registered the slam of her brother's door, a dim thud that dropped smoothly into the pounding of the bass.

CHAPTER TWENTY-FOUR

Why tonight? Why not any one of a thousand other nights over the past years? Why not tomorrow or next year or never?

I throw those questions in for your benefit. For my own part, I don't ask ridiculous questions like that. You're like squirrels: expending every ounce of energy burying nuts, whose location you promptly forget, while ferociously scolding every dog and cat and crow who approach whatever tree you happen to be inhabiting at the moment. Not only does so little of what you do better your chances of survival, most of it doesn't even peripherally impact them. Yet you're consumed by them, with all your noise and energy.

Similarly, you are forever asking the wrong questions.

In fact, you're so prone to it that you've gone so far as to elevate the question "why" as if it were the true question, the only one that really matters, the realm of philosophers and physicists. The problem there is that why is a linear question, and you are non-linear beings, living in a non-linear world.

But I digress. I only mentioned it because I knew you would.

Tad tried to do his homework, he really did. He pulled out his books and his laptop, his notebook and his pen. He went to the student portal and pulled up his assignments for the week. He put on a playlist and wished he could turn up the volume loud enough to drown out the voices he was sure to hear later below. But he didn't, because the rule was that if the music could be heard on the other side of the bedroom door, it was too loud. That meant that, for noise-dampening purposes, his music wasn't useful. But at least it served as a distraction.

Quiet persisted longer than he thought it would. Even after he heard Rachel's door close across the hall, an uneasy stillness seemed to hold the house in its grip. Tad tried to focus on the equations in front of him, but Rachel's odd proclamation niggled at him.

"Maybe I have to go, but I don't have to leave you with him."

Tad couldn't think of any good constructions to put on that declaration. He knew Rachel too well to take comfort in her melodrama. She might possess a finely-honed sense of the dramatic, but it was no substitute in her for will. And she took her role as big sister far more seriously than Hannah ever had. Tad figured Hannah had been broken long before he came along.

He couldn't remember a time when his oldest sister hadn't been a spectre trapped in an ill-fitting skin. Even her art frightened him. It was so much more alive than she was, as if the paint were truly her breath, and that rattling sound in her chest a mere poor facsimile of life. She was never unkind, merely absent, her eyes always blank when they looked on him. In a home of violence, Rachel had tried to refashion herself, Tad had tried to hide himself, but Hannah had made a complete escape long before she left the house. Tad wondered sometimes if now that she was well away, if she sometimes crept up behind those blank eyes and peered out on a world all new, or if she'd gotten so lost in that mind there was no way back.

Maybe partly in response to that complete abandonment, Rachel was a person entirely present. Instead of vanishing in plain sight, Rachel was unmistakable, unforgettable. Professional level make-up application and a brilliantly unique fashion sense saved her from her otherwise Goth sensibilities and turned out a creature somewhere between punk rock and anime. If her anime side was too adorable to believed, her punk would punch you in the throat till you found your faith. And while she lied with the usual skill and frequency of teenagers, if Rachel made you a promise, you could bet she'd keep it. So, Tad was reasonably anxious about exactly how she planned to keep this one.

Siblings interest me. Born automatically into competition for every resource, they nonetheless possess a weird fealty that seems unaffected by actual affection. I've seen siblings who can't stand to be in the same room with each other for more than ten minutes literally give their lives for each other. When estranged as adults, they carry that absence of the other around with them like a boulder in a bag that they can't unpack and won't leave behind. They keep secrets for each other that they never tell. And in some mysterious fashion, they belong to each other even more than they belong to their parents. It's a mysterious dynamic, one I don't guess I'll ever truly comprehend.

If you stretched the definition, you could say I have siblings of my own, spirits that, like me, burst into being at the same word from the same parent. That stretch renders the fit over-small, though — we angels are colder creatures and outsized for common company. But I enjoy playing observer to how you wear the affectation: it makes these choices I offer so much more interesting.

You might be tempted to think of Tad as a young man, being fourteen and all, but that's not really the case. Boys remain young so much longer than girls do, you know. Regardless of what your tropes teach you, girls are the realists, boys the idealists. They cling to dreams and fantasies so much longer. Maybe that's because, while they're slaying dragons and clearing post-apocalyptic towns on big screens, their sisters are measuring out their real, live blood in toilets and pads and accepting the reality that their bodies can produce and host a life entirely separate from its own. Maybe it's because boys will become men who need desperately to believe in fairy tales in order to be able to survive the expectations society holds for them, while girls must clean up the mess of those expectations. Maybe it's just a weird biological tic.

At any rate, Tad was a very young fourteen, a child who wanted more than anything to believe that his sister was wrong, that if he just kept to his room and kept his head down, everything would go back the way it was. He wanted the world to be quiet for a while. He wanted to forget that his father had hit him. He wanted to never worry that he'd hit him again. He wanted his bruises to fade before the next time he looked in the mirror. He wanted Rachel to keep being Rachel, and for everyone to just be okay.

It might seem strange that Tad wasn't defensive of his mom the same way he was defensive of his sister. But his world view was skewed from the start. In his world, there was nothing unusual or particularly wrong about his father hitting his mother. Unpleasant, sure. Anxiety-inducing, absolutely. Had Tad spent night after night crying under the blankets as a toddler and young child, listening in terror to the sounds from the other room? Most certainly. But his mother protected him too well, and his father not at all.

For most of his life, the fights — if you could call them that — had all taken place behind closed doors. Perdie had always been quick to retreat, mindful of drawing the wolf well away from the other sheep. And Matt had reasons of his own for not displaying his brutality in front of his children. He enjoyed the awe that fear inspired, but he still clung to the fiction that he was his family's benevolent tyrant. Whether he would have ever admitted it to himself in so many words, he knew the impact his violence would have on his children's hearts. So, by mutual agreement, Perdie and Matt kept their tussles out of sight.

Other than red eyes and winces, even the physical evidence of abuse was largely hidden. Matt never struck his wife on the face or where marks could easily be seen. Sometimes she wore long sleeves on hot summer days. So none of the children were confronted with bruises or abrasions on a regular basis. There had been the occasional broken bone that had to be addressed, but Perdie was always matter of fact about the injuries, brushing the pain aside and adopting ridiculous cover stories as if they couldn't possibly be doubted.

As the children had grown older, the farce grew increasingly strained. So perhaps fourteen was the perfect age to confront these terrors as a young man might have been compelled to do. But when Tad went downstairs that night, he wasn't going to defend his mother. He was going to prevent his sister from defending him. While Rachel lay quietly in her room, coldly planning her father's murder, Tad acted impetuously, rashly, his only thought to prove to Rachel that he didn't need defending. That he could stand up to their father on his own so she wouldn't worry. So she wouldn't do the very thing she intended to do.

Oh, his light was a beautiful thing as he headed out that bedroom door. All the years in that dark, bleak house had dimmed its furore, but that night it all but burst from his skin, a living flame of colour

and brilliance that was glorious to behold. His wasn't the choice I
was hoping for, of course. The most selfish path is always the one
that keeps your tread closest to mine. Funny how sometimes the acts
most purely motivated by love are the ones that lead to the most
calamity. Point to my team.

Adrenaline burned along his limbs as his long legs ate up
the stairs, a fine, powerful energy that promised the capacity
to meet and overcome any threat. Raised voices grew louder
as he hit the first floor, and he turned unerringly to his
parents' bedroom door.

He didn't slow down, slamming the door open with such
force it bounced back off the wall.

"Leave her alone!" he yelled, even as his eyes were still
taking in the scene.

His mom was curled on the floor in a foetal position, her
hands uselessly over her head, even though Matt never struck
her there. His father was kicking her in the back of the thighs,
his face red and contorted with rage, his fists balled as he
kicked her again and again. At Tad's intrusion, he spun
around, charging mindlessly for his son, as if Tad had been the
target he'd longed for all along.

"Tad, no!" Perdie cried, unfurling her body with some difficulty and struggling to her feet.

But it was too late for retreat, even if Tad had wanted to.
And Tad didn't want to. The other night, when he'd been the
one on the floor, and his father had been raining blows on his
ribcage, terror and shock and a bone-deep hurt that was so
much more powerful than the physical pain had immobilised
him, left him helpless against his father's attack. Matt had only
stopped in shock at his own actions after he'd flung Rachel
across the room when she'd come to her brother's rescue.

Tonight was different. Like most children of abuse, Tad

had absorbed the latest heartache with that peculiar equanimity borne of trauma. Tonight, Tad was the angry one, and he was not afraid.

Matt was bigger, meaner, and more experienced, though. He slammed into Tad, shoving him into the wall, and throwing a punch into Tad's already bruised ribs. Tad grunted heavily, but as he doubled over, he raised his knee sharply, connecting with Matt's groin with a satisfying grinding of bone against tissue. Matt staggered back, howling in agony.

Tad pressed his advantage, shoving his father farther back and throwing a mostly ineffective punch at his cheekbone. The sheer shock of being the one struck rather than the striker was enough to rouse Matt back to something resembling a fighting stance. Unfortunately, this was the moment that Perdie rushed forward, seizing Tad's arm and trying to drag him back.

"Don't, Tad. Please. Just go to your room," she begged, as if Matt wouldn't have just pursued him there.

Distracted, with his mother clinging to him, Tad was an easy mark.

"Fucking pussy," Matt snarled, bringing his own knee up.

Tad crumpled, pain bursting behind his eyes with such blackness he thought he was passing out. Perdie stood over him, but not for long. Matt punched her in the breast and shoved her off her son, kicking her hard in the ribs when she fell to the ground.

"Stay out of this," Matt growled at her. "He thinks he's a man, he can take a hit like a man."

He reached down and yanked his son to his feet. With a pain-filled yell, Tad lowered his head and charged into his father's chest, forcing him back. Matt wrapped his arms around Tad's chest, drawing his head in closer so his neck was bent so tightly that he struggled to breathe. Matt spun around, pressing Tad's buttocks into the wall where he was held in a vice between his father and the wall while Matt pounded his ribs with heavy fists.

Tad tried to spin out of his father's grip, but the adrenaline had faded, replaced with gritty pain and fear. His body felt sluggish, broken, as he tried to twist himself free. His father merely adjusted his hold and struck again.

"Had enough?" Matt ground out. "Or are you still feeling like a hero?"

Tad didn't bother answering. He did the only thing he could — he slid down. He knew his father's first move would be one of those bone-crushing kicks, and he was right. Tad didn't curl up this time, though. He rolled and leapt to his feet. He swallowed a gasp as he met his father's eyes: Matt was unrecognisable with rage, a blind, vicious beast of a man with no humanity glinting in his gaze. Pure murder shone in his face. Fear swamped Tad — fear and fatalism.

He threw another punch. Tad knew things had changed when his father punched him back. He heard the sickening impact of fist to nose, felt a terrific crack and the hot spurt of blood and agony.

"Stop! Stop! Matt, please!" Perdie was sobbing somewhere behind them.

"Shut up, bitch!" Another blow, this time splitting Tad's cheek. Tad lunged and closed his hands around his father's neck, but Matt only laughed, a horrible cackle, terrifying in its raw amusement, and plucked Tad's hands powerfully away. He punched Tad in the face a third time, and Tad staggered back, his vision muddying as confusion filled his mind.

"Matt, stop it! You're going to kill him!" Perdie pushed in front of her son.

Effortlessly, Matt swept her aside. She clawed at his arm,

leaving long red furrows, and he slammed her face with his fist. Her neck snapped back, and she dropped to the ground.

Tad didn't even think about what came next. His choice had been made the moment he left his room. That decision had set in motion a series of events from which there was no escaping now. Just as surely as Matt had been headed for this moment from the first day he made his choice to deliberately strike his wife.

Without turning his head, Tad reached across the night-stand and picked up the heavy, ornately carved iron lamp that rested there, its gentle glow suffusing the corner with light, as if darkness weren't everywhere in that room. He swung it at his father's head with every ounce of strength in his wiry body.

Matt was just turning from his wife's crumpled body back to his son. His startled expression of surprise and terror as that lamp hurtled toward his skull fixed upon his son. Tad would be forever haunted by that last look, that fleeting millisecond in which his father's eyes met his for the last time.

Iron and bone collided, and bone gave way. Matt crumbled slowly down, surprise becoming confusion.

Tad dropped the lamp. Shaky legs propelled him back, back, out of the room as his entire body was racked with shudders.

"Help," he muttered with numb lips. "Help. Help me. I need help."

Phone. His thoughts felt like sludge, rolling across his mind with painstaking slowness. He needed to get to his phone. Call for help. His gaze travelled to his mother's form, still unconscious on the floor past her husband's body. Tad wanted to check on her, wake her up, make sure she was okay, but he couldn't bring himself to go back in there. He was horrified by himself, undone. His teeth chattered.

He forced his feet across the floor to the stairs. For a long moment, he stood there, staring up, overcome by the certainty that he could never make it all the way to his room. Finally, he gave up, went down on all fours, and crawled up one step at a time. Once at the top, he leaned tiredly against the wall, trying to slow his breathing. He nearly jumped out of his skin when Rachel's door banged open, and she stood staring down at him, her mouth open in a perfect "O" of surprise.

It only took a split second for her eyes to sweep his battered face and busted knuckles, the blood spattered on his skin. An angry flush reddened her cheeks.

"That son of a bitch!" she spat, and Tad bleakly registered the bitter hatred in her voice. "I'm going to kill him."

She started to push past Tad, but he reached out and grabbed her ankle.

"I think I already did," he said weakly.

A broken wail rose from somewhere downstairs, and both teenagers started horribly at the sound.

"Police," Tad attempted coherence. "We need to call the police. 9-1-1."

Rachel stared at him for a long moment, her expression unreadable. Then she spun around and snatched her phone off the bed, her fingers flying over the screen.

Tad's gaze moved back across the hallway, toward his own bedroom door. It seemed like a lifetime ago he was on the other side of that door. The otherworldly wailing had stopped, and Tad could hear his mother's stumbling steps as she looked through the house, calling his name hesitantly into the silence. It didn't occur to him to answer her. Instead he was listening to his sister recounting their address to the voice on the other end of the phone.

"Yeah, we need police and an ambulance, too. My brother is hurt really bad. I don't know—"

She sounded so calm, Tad thought. He was afraid to speak himself, afraid that if he opened his mouth a howl would escape, a cry of grief and rage from the beast that was clawing at his skin from the inside.

"My mom is hurt, too," Rachel was saying. "My dad might be dead."

She clapped a hand over her mouth, her eyes widening.

CHAPTER TWENTY-FIVE

Perdie had come back into herself all at once, her brain still firing frantically in fight-or-flight mode. Heedless of the pain crying out from every cell in her body and the sick pounding in her head, she scrambled to her feet, her eyes taking in the scene in an instant that still somehow lasted too long. Against all odds, the iron lamp had fallen just right, the metal cage around the bare bulb propped on the carpet so that the light still shone crazily around the room. Matt lay on the floor, a hideous pool of blood spreading from his head. But the one thing Perdie sought most desperately — her son — was nowhere to be seen.

Fear thundered along her limbs, racing with dread for a finish line that Perdie would have done anything to avoid. She dropped back to her knees beside her husband. It took her three tries before she could persuade herself to touch his face, to turn his head toward her. She hated him so much — hated him for doing this to her children, hated him for reaching out to destroy them even when he was destroyed himself. She already knew from the amount of blood soaking into the carpet that it was too late, that he was dead or dying; but for the sake of her son she had to try.

Blood soaked into her knees and shins as she knelt there, silent tears pouring down her face. When she finally turned his face toward hers, she saw what she feared: staring eyes, already glassing over. Now more than ever he looked like an animal, a devourer, a predator who had been eating the flesh of her children for years now. And in the end, despairing of any help from her, her son had killed the predator.

At least, that was what she thought had happened. It was still possible that Rachel had come into the room, broken into the altercation, and picked up the lamp herself. Regardless of which child had acted, one of them at least was surely doomed. Even if the police found it self-defence, they'd have to live their entire lives with the knowledge that they'd had to kill their own father or be killed. Perdie couldn't find a way out of that for her children.

That was the wail Tad and Rachel heard from upstairs. Perdie didn't grieve for her husband; perhaps that would have come later, when she remembered how things had been in the beginning, when she might mourn the man he'd become and wonder why he'd pursued that path so deliberately, or if he had. But today, Perdie grieved only for her children.

She thought of the sweet babies they'd been, trusting and affectionate, and how that trust and affection had been broken and replaced day by day with doubt and fear and hesitancy. She thought of how the one refuge they should have in this world, their home, had become their prison, and she and their father their jailers. She thought about police interrogations and newspaper articles and the stares and points and jeers at school.

A new fury — this one cold where so much of the evening had been hot, hot and rushed — suffused her limbs with a deliberate precision. She rose swiftly to her feet, ignoring the tacky fabric clinging to her legs. She picked up the iron lamp, feeling its heft in her trembling arm.

"I swung the lamp," she whispered.

She staggered out the bedroom door, trying to propel her unstable limbs as quickly as she could up the stairs. She could hear Rachel's voice, eerily calm as she spoke to 911. She saw Tad, covered in blood, sunk against the wall in a huddle of bony limbs and ragged clothes. Fresh tears started as she sunk to her knees beside him, cradled his battered face in her hands, and turned his gaze toward hers.

"I swung the lamp," she whispered. "I swung the lamp."

Tad's dark brown eyes were cavernous, swallowed up in pupils as he stared at her with little comprehension.

"No," he managed faintly. "No, I did it. I hit him."

"Listen to me, baby," Perdie tried again, keeping her voice low, mindful of the open phone line. "I hit him. He was attacking you, and I hit him. It's self-defence. I won't be in trouble. Let me do this."

"He's dead, isn't he?" Tad's voice shook, its tenor unrecognisable as her son's.

Perdie bit her lip hard and nodded. "Don't worry, honey," she said inanely. "I'll fix this. I'll fix it. Just let me tell them I hit him. It'll be easier for me than it would be for you. And I should have hit him. I should have gotten there first, so you didn't have to."

Tad's eyes drifted away, so wide and so uncomprehending. Helplessly, Perdie wondered if it was too late, if Tad was too broken to save. Rachel stood in the doorway, still on the phone, and her next words to the dispatch operator caught Perdie's ear.

"I don't know how badly hurt he is. I'll go check—"

"No," Perdie intervened forcefully. "Give me the phone, honey. I'll talk to them. Just sit with your brother."

Rachel stared at her mother with an unreadable expression as she passed over the phone. Perdie clutched it to her ear, ignoring how the phone slipped in her palm, damp with blood and sweat.

"This is Perdie Blevins," she said as clearly as she could, trying to control the shaking in her voice. "I've just killed my husband. My son needs medical attention. My husband was attacking him ... I don't know how badly hurt he is, but there's blood everywhere."

"You say you've killed your husband?"

"Yes, ma'am."

"Is there a gun or other weapon in the house?"

"No, no, nothing like that. I — I picked up a lamp and hit him over the head with it."

"And you said your son is injured. Is he conscious?"

"Yes, yes, he's awake. He's here with me."

"Is anyone else injured? Your daughter Rachel I was just speaking with?"

"No, no, she's not hurt. I mean — I'm injured, too, but I'll be fine. I'll be fine."

"All right, ma'am, the EMTs and the police are on the way. Can you hear the sirens?"

"Yeah, I think so. I'm going to go open the door."

"Okay, just stay on the line with me while—"

But Perdie had already disconnected.

"Stay here. Help is coming," Perdie said to her children. She pressed a hard kiss to each of their foreheads. Rachel had been watching her intently while she spoke into the phone, her tight expression giving nothing away. Tad still looked lost, disconnected. "Don't worry. There will be a lot of questions.

Tell them I told you not to say anything. I'll handle this. I'll fix it."

Perdie went down the stairs, her knees quaking as all the frenzy that had carried her this far left her body in a whoosh. As she opened the front door and the cold, November dark rushed over her, she saw the flash of blue and red approaching. She raised her hands over her head and went down to her knees. She didn't know if that's what they wanted, but she didn't want to give the police any excuse to storm the house and frighten the kids any more than they already were.

Panic beat behind her eyes and threatened to overcome her as she struggled to see past the drifting snowflakes that seemed to catch and toss every prism of colour from the lights. Someone was approaching, she could hear a voice yelling at her, but her brain had lost its power to translate sounds into thoughts.

"I'm Perdie Blevins," she yelled into the chaos that might have all been only in her head. "I killed my husband. My kids are inside. They need help."

The hands that snapped restraints around her wrists and lifted her to her feet were brusque but, surprisingly, not unkind. She was drawn out of the porchlight and into the streetlight, her eyes still caught in the hurly-burly of the ambulance and police lights. She sensed rather than saw multiple people rushing past her, into the house.

"Upstairs," she managed to say to the faceless uniform holding her arm. "The kids are upstairs. Matt is downstairs, in the bedroom."

He — she? — relayed the information into a crackling radio on her shoulder. "You're covered in blood," said the officer in a low voice, pitched for her ears and somehow carrying across the madness erupting on what had been her quiet, suburban lawn. "Are you injured also?"

"Yes," Perdie answered. Pain washed over her suddenly, a rush of sensation that made her head swim and her stomach pitch. "What's going to happen to the kids? They don't have to go to the police station, do they? I don't want them to go to the police station."

The officer — Perdie was pretty sure it was a woman now — drew her over to the back of a waiting ambulance and sat her on the open tailgate, directing an EMT to check her out. Perdie tried to keep her eyes on the officer, but she was swallowed up in the night that waited just on the edge of the ambulance interior lights.

"We'll see what their medical needs are first. Minors can't be questioned without their parents or attorney present, so we can wait to get their statements. Is there someone I can call to come get them?"

"Julie," Perdie managed through stiffening lips, trying not to cry out as the EMT examined her injuries. "Julie Chambers will come. I can give you her number."

"You're going to want this one to get cleared at the hospital," the EMT said over Perdie's head. "There's pretty severe abdominal bruising. May be internal bleeding or broken ribs."

CHAPTER TWENTY-SIX

"I'm Ella," I said softly, adjusting the IV cord. Perdie looked like she'd been run over by a train. Her face was bruised and swollen, her hair matted and bloody, her skin sallow beneath the bloom of abrasions. Her lids rested at half-mast, the product of exhaustion rather than any pain relief. Her wrists were manacled to the bed rail. Beside her sat the police officer, an expressionless woman with chestnut hair pulled back into a bun. She was scrolling through her phone, offering Perdie and me the illusion of privacy, though I could sense her listening to every word and keeping a peripheral eye on our activities.

"Perdie," Perdie managed, the force of civility breaking through trauma.

Just one more interesting way you cling to your definitions of yourself.

"We're going to do some imaging, make sure that you don't have any hidden injuries we can't see on the surface. Although it looks like you have more than enough to deal with just on the surface. Are you in a lot of pain?"

Perdie nodded.

"Once we know what we're looking at, we'll work on relieving some of that pain. In the meantime, can I get you anything? Something to drink, maybe?"

Perdie's eyes sparked, and I knew that she hadn't even realised how thirsty she was till I mentioned it. I held out the cup with the plastic bendy straw, and she hunched her head painfully forward, sucking eagerly at the water.

"Are the restraints necessary?" I asked the officer.

Of course, I knew they were, but nurses and doctors are always suckers for anyone in pain.

"She murdered her husband," the officer returned drily without looking up from her phone. "So, yes. The restraints stay. I'll go with you to imaging, take them off, and then put them back on when we come back."

"Based on what I can see of your face," I said to Perdie, as if the officer weren't there, "I'd say he had it coming."

I sensed Perdie trying to curve her lips into a weak smile, but she abandoned the effort before a single muscle twitched.

"I should have left," she muttered. "I should have left ten years ago. A thousand times since then, I guess, but ten years ago I made the decision that it was somehow worth it, somehow better for my kids, if I stayed. And I stuck by that decision. And now we're here. And my kids—"

Her voice broke, and tears welled up and squeezed out between the swollen flesh of her eyelids.

I tucked in the blanket and injected just the right amount of scepticism into my voice. "Better for your kids?"

Perdie shook her head weakly. "I know — now — how

crazy that sounds. But I didn't want my kids to grow up in a broken home, with a mother who was never home. I didn't want them to grow up in poverty and maybe never have a chance at a real education. I thought I could … manage … this side of things and keep it from affecting them."

From the corner of my eye, I saw the officer's jaw tighten. I wondered if she were a single mom herself. Her sympathy for her captive thrummed in the room like a living thing, beating to be free of the uniform that bound her fealty to the law only.

"Well, if it was self-defence — and it looks like it was — I'm sure you'll be out of these handcuffs and back with your kids in no time. The police have processes they have to follow, but they don't have any interest in charging an innocent person. Try to be patient. You'll be home before you know it."

I knew how empty a consolation I offered. In fact, I was counting on it.

Sure enough, Perdie summoned a hollow bark of a laugh. "Home? What's home? There's blood on the carpet. My son — my son …" Her voice trailed off as she swallowed convulsively. "My children have no home. No peace. I've destroyed them. I've broken them and I don't know how to fix them. I was the one person … my only job was protecting them, and see what I've done?"

Now we were coming to it. Just like last time. How easily you talk yourselves into it. How quickly you think you have any real power to change. The more God-like you imagine yourself, the more in control, the more responsible, the closer you are to me. And again, I was ready.

"What could you possibly have done?" My voice was soft,

almost tender. The police officer leaned in unconsciously, hanging on the words she was pretending not to hear.

"I could have saved them. I could have left that day, ten years ago. I would give anything — anything — to take back that choice. I wish to God I'd left. I'd give up everything, everything, to have left."

That's all I needed to hear.

THE ACCIDENT

CHAPTER TWENTY-SEVEN

Sometimes even I feel it, that rush of overwhelming grief and loss that defines so much of your experience. I can never quite decide if it's a terrible sensation or a wonderful one. It's foreign, alien, to me now, that longing after what has passed beyond me, but still it awakens a memory of what I once was that, while aching in its nostalgia, is somehow marvellous. I don't grieve anymore, you see. Why would I? When loss threatens, I simply move to another pleasure, another delight, and feed my being. I refuse to suffer ever again. At least, I try to refuse. Sometimes, like this time, it intrudes, and the sweetness of the agony flames my hunger like a drug.

We've come full circle, as it happens. Given a choice, you will almost always take whatever is other, convinced that it will be better. That somehow your singular choice is the fulcrum on which the whole universe rests. Feeding that delusion strengthens my grip on you. As long as the spiritual world offers you shame and guilt and despair, my world is the hopeful place to which you turn for comfort.

I could have moved on. There was no choice here, in this dark, hot place of twisted metal and blood and fear. Nothing that should have held me here as witness. But I was held, nonetheless, rooted in place as each ragged, slowing breath spun universes of light and colour.

Rachel's eyes were closed, a cobwebbed sheet of glass lying on her face and distorting the lashes resting on her cheeks. By the time she woke, her brother would be gone; but for now, Tad and I were alone together in the dark and the cold.

Car headlights shot crazily across the open field, illuminating the gentle drift of sparkling snowflakes as they attempted to blanket this violence of speed and metal in clouds of white. The twisted car sighed and hissed, every now and then emitting a wrenching heave as it struggled to settle its distorted frame. Outside, bare skin freezing to the ice that coated the ground, Tad lay under the stars.

Later, when his step-father bore the burden of identifying his son, he wouldn't recognise his face. But as I lay beside him and watched his frosty breaths slow, all I saw was light. Glorious light. The light that had always been his own, the light he'd clung to and chosen no matter his circumstances. Amazingly, as he lay there in a completely shattered heap of bones and muscle and blood, his eyes were open, fixed on the dark sky above.

He couldn't see the stars, of course. A greyness bore down on him, the weight of the clouds that brought the snow, a dimmer blackness against the night sky. But I think he could feel the gaze of those stars all the same, cutting through those wisps of vapour, could feel that ancient light that had travelled so far to meet his own for just this moment in time.

Awful sounds whispered out his broken windpipe every once in a while. It would be a long time before emergency vehicles arrived. The only witnesses to the accident were lying here in this field, one dying, one unconscious, one fighting to live.

I can't explain the impulse, but as with all my impulses, I acted on it, slipping my hand into his own. His fingers were limp, caked with blood. I closed my eyes, imagining that I could fill his cooling form with my own warmth. Slowly, I became aware that I was not the only creature holding him. Another sat on his other side, silent and waiting.

It was the Angel of Death, of course. As I watched, wordless, he quietly and steadily wound the brilliant thread of Tad's light on to his spool. He didn't acknowledge me, which came as no surprise. He had made his choice long ago, as had I, and he would not revisit it. I might as well have been invisible to him.

It seemed to take forever. I couldn't tear my eyes away from those shimmering colours, sparkling and glowing against the black night, against Tad's blanching skin, against the darkness pressing behind my own eyes. I felt as much as saw when that last particle, that last wave, unwound from Tad's soul and wrapped securely around the Angel's spool.

By the time the sweet, bright light I'd tried not to chase for so long had found its way home, other, harsher lights had intruded: spinning blue and red, sweeping white, the pallid efforts of men to illuminate a night they barely comprehended.

While Tad was taken to the ambulance, I stayed in that field to bear a little longer witness. Rachel's still-senseless form in the car was the nearest companion I apprehended as firefighters struggled to free her from the tangle of steel and glass. Unreasonably angry, I pushed back at a night impossibly dark, oppressive and hateful and empty. Push as I might, there came no answering shove, no meeting of force to force.

This is the absence, the emptiness, I always fight to silence now. It's not that God are my enemy. It's that They don't even acknowledge me anymore. I am become my own annihilation, and even the darkness does not know my name.

I didn't stay there, of course. I have no interest in pursuing my own pain. When something hurts, I soothe it. When I'm hungry, I eat. Thirsty, I drink. Angry, I kill. What else is there? This predilection for standing in the room of pain is a human tendency for which I have no interest.

CHAPTER TWENTY-EIGHT

All in all, not one of my more impressive wins. I only walked away with Matt in the end. And what a hollow victory that was. Hardly worth the fight. He's little more than an empty belly, after all, and those can scarcely provide much entertainment in the dark realms where I must one day retreat. Perhaps I'll get lucky, and that'll turn out to be a fiction as much for my own sake as everyone else's. I'd prefer silence, I think. Just sleep, to the absence of all light and colour and hope.

A surprising terminus, when given all the many opportunities the others had to embrace my world. Perdie mistakenly thought that one choice could dictate destiny, but that's not true at all. Sure, I had her for a minute when she opted for money and security over freedom and happiness, but even her poor choices following that were motivated by love. Rachel was ready to sacrifice her own future to save her brother, and Tad did sacrifice himself to save her. And I never had much of a chance with Reilly. He'd chosen the spiritual life over the material long ago, and with or without Perdie in his life, he'd have continued on that path.

It's not over, though. I do love the preposterous set-ups your fables and fairy tales propose, the notion that selling your soul to the devil is a one-time proposition. Just as I can lose my hold over you at any time, you let me regain it at any time, too. Retreating, regrouping, is all part of the battle plan. I honestly enjoy the diversity of attacks some of you merit. I'll happily surrender back your precious self, on another day when you least expect me, if it wins me another skirmish. It would almost be anti-climactic when the fiercest of you lose, if I didn't have an endless supply of ready, reckless souls to rush on to. Lucky me. I'd hate to miss you when you extinguish.

To be fair, I suspect that even with the loss of their son, Perdie and Reilly will hold on to each other over me. But Rachel and Hannah both still offer a plethora of opportunities for me to stake my claim. We shall see.

It frustrates you, doesn't it? You wanted a different ending. You wanted all this to mean something. You wanted an answer to a question you can't even frame properly. But here's the thing:

I'm not the teacher. I'm the test. I have nothing to teach you. No judgement to hand down.

So, I'm sorry if you thought, somehow, I was going to make everything better for Perdie. If you thought, like she did, that there was some series of choices she could make that would guarantee her children's happiness or even just their survival. I'm the devil, remember? I was never going to spin this into a happy ending for you. You can only make that yourself. The fact that it all ends proves that I'm right — there is no happiness. There is only fleeting pleasure. And pain. So choose pleasure when you can. Because the pain is inescapable when it advances.

I'm sorry, too, if you thought I would somehow save Tad. He was already saved, you see, and was always out of my reach.

Which brings me to you, and your own peculiar light. Trim your wick, lift your shade. Cast that shine a little closer. I do get weary of the darkness.

ACKNOWLEDGEMENTS

Ella is undeniably a slippery creature, and as much as I appreciate her willingness to share her story with me, I sometimes found it impossibly cryptic to decipher. To that end, I am immeasurably grateful to my editors Samantha Brace and Peyton Stableford for the sleepless nights and long days they spent helping me chip away the detritus and deceit from the fairy tale that finally emerged.